THE
YELLOW COTTAGE
VINTAGE MYSTERIES

AN
ACCIDENTAL
MURDER

BOOK 1

J. NEW

BOOKS BY J. NEW

The Yellow Cottage Vintage Mysteries in order:

The Yellow Cottage Mystery (Free)
An Accidental Murder
The Curse of Arundel Hall
A Clerical Error
The Riviera Affair
A Double Life

The Finch & Fischer Mysteries in order:

Decked in the Hall
Death at the Duck Pond

For Mum with Love.

AN
ACCIDENTAL
MURDER

CHAPTER ONE

I t was a particularly chilly and damp Saturday afternoon in September, and I was taking a momentary break from the unpacking of boxes to have a quick sandwich and a cup of tea. I'd already laid and lit the log fire and now sat, sleepy and content, in an overstuffed armchair, watching the flames dance and flicker in the grate. And listening to the wind whistling down the chimney like an irate ghost.

I'd only been living in the cottage for a few short weeks, but it felt as though I'd lived there all my life. From the moment I stepped inside at the initial viewing, it had wrapped itself around me like a second skin and I knew I'd come home at last.

It had—or so I thought at the time—been a spur-of-the-moment decision to come back to the island after so many years. But it seemed now as though fate had conspired to steer my actions.

As a child, my family had chosen the island as a holiday destination for two weeks each summer. And one year—the last as it happened—I'd seen and fallen in love with The Yellow Cottage.

Coming back so many years later on a whim, I had discovered it was for sale and, to cut a long story short, I bought it.

As I sat there drinking my tea, remembering the rather strange circumstances in which the cottage had become my home, the cat came in. Not a particularly interesting event in itself, I'd agree, except this cat walked in through a solid wall.

I'd idly been wondering why he always chose that particular spot to enter from the back garden, but once I knew the answer it was obvious. I was cleaning the small snug area under the stairs a couple of days ago, having decided it would be a perfect place to use as an office.

Going through the bookshelves, I'd come across a large hardback book, and folded inside were some of the old building plans. Looking closer, I realised that the current door to the back wasn't the original. That had been bricked up and a new opening made further along. Phantom, as I'd named the cat in a particularly unimaginative moment, was using the old doorway. The same one I expect he always used when he'd lived there as a flesh and blood companion.

Phantom was a legacy from Mrs. Rose, the previous owner. She and I had met when I first came to view the cottage a few months ago, and we had chatted briefly whilst simultaneously saving a swan from *'death-by-fishing-line.'* It wasn't until I returned to the cottage and Mr. Wilkes, the patiently waiting estate agent, that I found out she'd already been dead for seven months.

As it turned out, Phantom wasn't the only thing Mrs. Rose had left me. But it wasn't until the phone rang and set in motion a series of extraordinary events that I realised just how strange the rest of my life was going to be.

It took a minute to find the phone, entombed as it was under a pile of linen and, for some bizarre reason, three odd mittens and a teapot. But eventually I pulled it free and picked up the receiver.

"Hello?"

"Ella, it's Jerry. How are you settling in? Everything unpacked?"

I laughed. "Not exactly, Jerry. That's why I was so long answering the phone actually. I'm still knee deep in boxes and can't find a thing."

"Well, you certainly sound happy about it."

"Like the proverbial pig in muck. It's wonderful. You and Ginny really must come and visit, especially now I'm so much closer to London. You could get the train and be here in under an hour. I can't remember the last time we were all together."

"Actually, that's why I'm calling. Ginny is pining for her sister-in-law and wants you to come for lunch tomorrow. Can you make it?"

"Of course I can make it, I'd love to come. Just so long as you don't expect me to dress up. Considering how the unpacking is going I may turn up wearing my dressing gown and Wellingtons."

"Well, I doubt Ginny and I would bat an eyelid. We're used to your odd little ways—not sure how Peter would feel though." He laughed.

"Oh, very funny, you make me sound like some eccentric octogenarian. Wait a minute…who's Peter?"

"Oh, didn't I mention he was coming too?"

"Jerry, you know very well you didn't." I sighed. "Promise me you aren't matchmaking again. You know what an utter disaster your last attempt was!"

"*Moi?* How could you think such a thing of your dear brother?"

"You really are the most awful liar, you know. Please don't, Jerry. It makes me feel so uncomfortable, and it's not necessary. I'm perfectly happy as I am. More so since I moved here actually. If it happens then it happens, but I'm not going to force it. And I'm certainly not going to be paraded in front of your friends like a prize heifer, no matter how well-intentioned you are."

"Oh, Ella, I'm sorry. I really didn't mean to upset you. I just want you to be happy. It's been a few years since John died and I don't think you've been on more than three dates the entire time. I just worry about you, that's all."

"Jerry, I'm not upset, truly, and I *am* happy. I know you worry, but everything really is wonderful. In fact, I've already made a new friend. Her name is Mini. She lives just up the lane and she's a potter! Can you imagine? She makes the most glorious things and looks like a film star. She's away visiting relatives at the moment, but I'd love for you and Ginny to meet her. You'll see tomorrow that I'm perfectly fine. We'll chat then, all right? I'll get the 11:00am train and should be at your door just after noon."

"I'll meet you off the train, Ella."

I smiled at his concern. It was hard to believe *I* was the elder of the two of us.

"Jerry, you live a fifteen-minute walk from the station. I'll be fine."

"Darling, if you're going to wander the streets of London in your dressing gown, then I need to be there to prevent you from being carted away and thrown in a padded room. I'll be there waiting. You'll recognise me by the rose in my lapel and I'll be carrying a copy of the Times."

I grinned. Jerry wrote spy thrillers and he loved the clichés.

I dropped my voice to a whisper, "What's the password?"

"Snowmen in winter are a wondrous sight, but beware the yellow one."

I laughed out loud. "Silly ass. I'll see you tomorrow," I said and hung up.

I spent the next two hours sifting through boxes in an attempt to find something suitable to wear. I would have loved to turn up in my dressing gown—the look on Jerry's face would have been priceless and he'd have appreciated the joke—but with a stranger at lunch, I thought better of it.

Eventually, I found a suitable dress, a wrap and boots. With those items set aside, I searched for and miraculously found, in less than half an hour, my jewellery case, and the ensemble was complete.

I was looking forward to seeing Jerry and Ginny again and a Sunday lunch sounded divine. I'd barely made a dent in unpacking the kitchen items since moving in. As long as I had the necessities like tea, I considered it a job well done. I just hoped that this Peter chap wasn't expecting it to be more than it was.

But as it turned out, that was to be the least of my worries.

CHAPTER TWO

I adore train journeys. There's something soporific about the constant clickety-clack of the wheels on the track, the gentle swaying motion, and the speeding by of minute life outside the window.

My carriage was very quiet; there were only two other passengers besides myself. A gentleman with his head stuck in a newspaper and a woman with a cat in a basket on the seat beside her.

Seeing the woman with the cat reminded me of Phantom. One of the many bonuses to having a ghost for a pet was that I hadn't had to arrange for anyone to come in and feed him. As far as I could tell he didn't eat; well, not on my plane of existence anyway. He also didn't leave half-eaten presents for me on the doorstep. He didn't leave hair everywhere or cough up fur balls either, which was a blessing.

I hadn't found it at all odd when he'd walked through the wall that first time. I suppose it was because I'd almost come to expect it, especially after the stories Mr. Wilkes had told me, along with the fact that I'd had a perfectly normal conversation with a woman who had been dead for several months.

I suppose I should have felt more rattled than I did, but for some reason I didn't. It all seemed perfectly ordinary and I found I could just accept it for what it was.

What I did find curious, though, was that Phantom could choose to be solid almost at will. He'd curled up on my lap last evening and let me stroke him and he was as solid as I was. I could feel his weight on my knee and his soft fur under my fingers. I could even feel the gentle vibration in his chest as he purred contentedly, although all of this was done in complete silence. Ghost cats obviously didn't make any noise.

Then, hopping off a little while, later he took on a sort of transparent quality and disappeared through the wall into the garden. I wondered if all spirits could do that. And if they could, were we surrounded by ghosts who appeared to be just as alive as we were yet we didn't know it? I don't suppose we'd know until they decided to walk through a wall.

I hadn't told anyone about Phantom or Mrs. Rose. The only one that knew was Mr. Wilkes, and seeing as though he'd had some unexplained experiences himself, I knew he understood.

I had toyed with the idea of mentioning it to Mini, but as the friendship was new, I didn't want to ruin it by talking about spirits and have her run for the hills. It would be nice to have someone to talk to about it though.

I was still pondering the mystery of it all when the train pulled into the station.

As I walked up the platform, I could see Jerry beyond the barrier. He was wearing a rose in his lapel and carrying a copy of the Times under his arm. I couldn't believe it; I should have worn my dressing gown after all.

As I approached, I sidled up beside him facing the opposite direction and said in a most serious voice, "Snowmen in winter are a wondrous sight."

"Yes but beware the yellow one," he replied.

Unlike the carriage, the station was very busy, and we were awarded several bemused glances as we burst into raucous laughter and made our way outside.

Linking my arm into Jerry's, I said, "So … tell me about your friend Peter. What does he do and how did you meet him?"

By the time we reached the apartment I knew as much about Peter Clairmont as Jerry did.

He'd not known him for long, just a matter of weeks actually. They'd met via a mutual acquaintance—at a fund-raising dinner that Jerry had attended—and found they had something in common, namely Jerry's books. It turned out Peter was a fan, and not only that but he was also an aspiring writer and had picked Jerry's brains all night.

As we stepped through the apartment door, I was engulfed in a perfumed hug.

"Ella, it's wonderful to see you. It's been far too long. I'm thrilled you could come to lunch."

Ginny, as always, was impeccably groomed. The only child of minor aristocracy, she and Jerry had fallen in love quickly and passionately, much to her father's chagrin. Jerry's books were being published by a small independent press at the time and consequently his income wasn't much. Ginny's father felt she could and should do better, but Ginny was adamant she was going to follow her heart.

For the first couple of years they lived on Ginny's trust fund and with the time and freedom to write, along with the support, belief and encouragement from his new wife, Jerry produced not one, but two best-sellers, and their future was assured. Needless to say, Ginny's father had a complete turn-about of opinion and became one of Jerry's staunchest supporters. To hear him talk now you'd think *he'd* been the one to launch Jerry's career.

"Ginny, how lovely to see you," I said. "It really has been too long. A Sunday lunch is just what I needed. I've barely unpacked the kitchen at the cottage."

As she took my wrap and hung it in the closet, I walked down the hallway and entered the kitchen with Jerry and Ginny on my heels.

"Oh!" I said as I spied a ball of fur curled up on a cushion. "You've got a ... " I froze. It was a cat—but not just any cat—it was Phantom. What on earth was he doing here? I knew Ginny would never have a cat—she had allergies.

I realised I was mid-sentence and they were waiting to see what I would say, so I foolishly pushed on regardless, "Lovely view," then looked up to see the ugly wall of the adjacent building staring at me from the window.

I could feel the heat of the blush suffusing my neck and rising to my cheeks. *Ella, you idiot, how are you going to get yourself out of this one?* I was just about to open my mouth and dig the hole a little deeper, when Jerry saved the day by bursting into laughter.

"Sarcasm, Ella? You must be feeling better. I agree the view is appalling from this window but the rest are wonderful. It's a small price to pay for the location, though. Come, let's go through to the drawing-room and I'll pour us some drinks."

Following Jerry, I glanced back at Phantom, who had extricated himself from the chair and was now padding along silently behind me. If I had any doubt the others couldn't see him it was allayed when we entered the drawing room. He jumped up on to the table right in front of us, and nonchalantly walked its entire length as though he owned the place before settling on the window ledge. Neither Gerry nor Ginny flinched. They really couldn't see him.

I was just hoping that I wouldn't make more of a fool of myself than I already had when the doorman buzzed up to say their guest had arrived. It was time to meet Peter Clairmont. I could only hope Phantom would remain invisible to everyone.

CHAPTER THREE

I hadn't really given a thought to what Peter Clairmont would be like, but as he entered the drawing room with Jerry, I caught Phantom out of the corner of my eye. He was standing with his back arched and his fur on end, his mouth open in a silent hiss and teeth bared menacingly. I glanced back as Jerry made the introductions. Peter seemed harmless enough and was quite pleasant both to look at and in his manner, but Phantom obviously didn't like him at all. I wondered if this was some sort of warning. Could Peter be the reason Phantom was here?

As we all took our seats in the dining-room and the first course was served, the conversation turned to how Jerry and Peter had met. I hadn't realised Ginny hadn't met Peter either, although like me she knew the circumstances of their meeting.

"Well, of course Jerry was extremely generous with both his time and his money at the fundraiser, you know," Peter began. "I must say we raised a terrific amount for the orphanage that night;

it was more successful than I dared to hope and will keep us going for a good few months. Jerry was actually the one that got the ball rolling with the first donation. After that it was simply a matter of collecting the loot, so to speak."

Ginny patted her husband's arm and smilingly said, "Well, of course he was, he's the most generous man I know."

"How did you get involved with the orphanage?" I asked, studiously ignoring Phantom, who had taken up residence at the foot of Peter's chair and was staring at him, unblinking.

"Actually, it was my home for a short while. I felt it only right when I reached adulthood to I gave back to those who provided a roof over my head when I needed it most."

Phantom bared his teeth. I ignored him. What on earth was the matter with him?

"Well, that's very commendable, Peter, I must say. We could do with more people like you in the world," said Jerry.

As the dishes were removed and the next course set, I asked Peter what sort of books he wrote.

"Nothing like the fabulous spy thrillers that Jerry pens. I write historical novels mostly, although I'm sure he told you I've yet to actually publish anything."

"Well, I'm sure Jerry would be only too happy to help in that direction, wouldn't you, darling?" Ginny said.

"Of course. Let me know when you're ready and I'll put you in touch with my agent. I can't promise anything, mind you, but it's worth a shot."

Peter smiled, obviously pleased, as I would be in his position.

"That's very kind of you, Jerry. I'll certainly take you up on that offer when I'm ready."

As the main course was taken away and the most fabulous Pavlova arrived in its place, talk moved onto more mundane things and I switched off as I attacked my dessert with gusto. I had always had a sweet tooth and this was one of my favourites.

Phantom had barely moved since we sat down and was still giving Peter the stink-eye. He was like one of those Egyptian statues and I just caught myself in time before I mentioned it. Honestly, it was quite hard work pretending everything was normal when I was the only one who could see the spirit of a cat walking about.

I looked up, having finished my Pavlova, to find everyone staring at me.

"What are you all looking at? Do I have cream on my nose or something?"

I started furiously dabbing at my face with my handkerchief just in case.

Ginny squealed with delight. "No, of course not, silly. Peter was just asking about your cottage and you were ignoring him."

"I wasn't ignoring him, Ginny! I didn't hear him, that's all." Turning to Peter, I said, "I do apologise. I was miles away. What would you like to know?"

"Come on, we'll have coffee in the drawing-room and you can tell Peter all about the cottage," said Jerry.

Comfortably ensconced on the sofa, with Peter at a polite distance next to me and Phantom perched on the arm, still staring at him with complete and utter hostility, I told him the story of how I had come by the cottage and bought it, long after Jerry and I used to holiday there as children. I made it all sound as normal as possible, no mention of ghostly owners or exploding pantries, and absolutely no mention of spectral cats. This must have annoyed Phantom as he shot his paw out and caused me to spill hot coffee all down my dress.

"Oh, Phantom!" I exclaimed as I jumped up.

"Now there's a curse word you don't hear every day," laughed Jerry. "I'll have to remember that for my next book."

At that, we all burst out laughing. To be honest, I still felt like a prize idiot but Jerry, as usual, pulled the embarrassing attention away from me, for which I was very grateful.

After managing to clean up as much as I could in the cloakroom, I returned to announce that it was time for me to catch my train home.

"I'll walk you to the station," Peter said, standing. "I'm heading that way. That's if you don't mind?"

So, with that settled, we thanked Jerry and Ginny for a wonderful lunch and departed with promises we'd get together again soon. Little did I know it would be sooner than I expected.

"So you and Jerry used to holiday on the island when you were children?" Peter asked as we made our way to the station.

I nodded.

"I remember one time at the orphanage we had a day trip down there. It was the first time many of us had seen the sea."

"Do you mind me asking how you ended up there?" I asked. I didn't want to appear nosy, especially if he didn't like to talk about it, but I was dying to know.

"No, I don't mind you asking. I don't normally make a habit of discussing it, but you're actually very easy to talk to," he smiled. I blushed, thinking that he was actually quite a nice man. Not good looking in a movie star sort of way, and slightly on the short side, but he had a kind face.

Phantom, trotting beside me, turned and hissed at him again as though he were reading my thoughts. I ignored him and turned back to Peter as he continued.

"My parents were killed in an accident when I was nine. My only next of kin were an Aunt and Uncle, but they'd moved to Ireland before I was born. I didn't know them, although I had heard my mother mention a sister. I think they must have been estranged, as I'd never known them to be in contact. It took the authorities a while to trace them, and during the interim period I was sent to the orphanage to live."

"How long were you there?"

"Just short of four months, but it was summer and we were allowed to play outside a lot and it wasn't as cold inside as it is in the winter. Part of the funds raised recently will go towards an overhaul of the heating system. Plus we had a day trip to the seaside when funds would allow. I think I went twice during my stay which was unheard of. Although after the last one the visits were stopped for a while."

"Oh? What happened?"

He sighed, and his face took on a sad cast.

"One of the girls waded out too far and a rip-tide took her. There was nothing any one could have done."

I stopped, my hand on my heart. "Oh, Peter, how awful. That must have been so traumatic for you and the other children to witness … and that poor girl."

"Well, that's part of the reason why I help. If there had been some-one there with training, then I'm sure she could have been saved."

By this point, we'd reached the ticket collector and would have to part ways. "I'm terribly sorry if I opened up old wounds, but thank you for sharing your story with me, and I'm glad you finally found your extended family," I said.

"Well, that's a story for another time," he said with a frown. "It's been a pleasure, Ella. Perhaps we could do it again sometime?"

I sighed inwardly. I hated being put on the spot like this. He'd been a perfect gentleman all through lunch, so I was inclined to believe Jerry when he said he wasn't matchmaking. Even so, there was something holding me back. A niggle of doubt like an itch I couldn't scratch. "Well that's very kind of you, Peter. You never know. Perhaps we'll have lunch with Jerry and Ginny again," I said, smiling and shaking his hand as I presented my ticket to the guard.

I left Peter at the barrier and made my way down the platform. A quick glance down told me Phantom was determined to accompany me on the train.

As I got on and turned right to enter the carriage, he shot in front of me and sat in the doorway preventing me from going any further. Well, even I understood that message, so I turned around and went in the other carriage.

Phantom jumped up on one of the seats and looked at me.

"No, I can't sit there. I have to have my back to the engine otherwise it makes me feel queasy."

"I know what you mean, dear," said a voice.

Oh, good grief. I must have spoken out loud. I looked over and saw the voice belonged to a lady a few seats down. Nodding and smiling, I took the seat opposite Phantom and popped a mint in my mouth. Hopefully that would help me to keep it shut.

Just as the first whistle blew, a child no more than eight years-old shot into the carriage and scrambled under the seat in front of me, obviously hiding. I looked down the aisle, but saw no one chasing her. Glancing out of the window, I saw that all was perfectly quiet on the platform too. I looked back at her, opening my mouth to speak, but she put a finger over her lips to shush me. The pleading look and abject fear in her eyes made me keep quiet.

The carriage began to fill up as people took their seats, but the girl was well hidden, tiny as she was, and luckily no one noticed her. I was having second thoughts about keeping my mouth shut when the train began to pull out of the station. It was then that I noticed Phantom had disappeared.

CHAPTER FOUR

The girl remained hidden the entire journey. As people got on and off the train, the sea of faces in front of me changed and I was awarded a glimpse of her periodically during the brief moments when the seat was empty. She lay there as quiet as a mouse and perfectly still. She'd look at me every now and then and each time she raised a finger to her lips. Eventually, I watched as her eyelids grew heavy and she fell asleep, no doubt lulled by the swaying of the train and the sound of the wheels on the track.

I took this chance to examine her in more detail. Her dark trousers were homespun wool and, although clean, were far too big for her and had been rolled up several times at the cuff. Her shoes, whilst looking to be the correct size, were scuffed and worn through so her sock could be clearly seen through the sole of one. Her navy coat was the right size and looked warm, which was a blessing, but I thought she could have done with a hat as it was bitterly cold out, especially at this time of night. I wondered what her story was. She was obviously either from a very poor family or she was homeless—a runaway perhaps? I wondered what sort of tragedy would befall a family to result in a tiny child like this having to curl up under a train seat. She should be home, tucked up safe and warm and sleeping the sleep of the innocent.

My station was the last on the line and by the time we pulled up the carriage was empty. As we stopped, the girl opened her eyes and then carefully unfolded herself from beneath the seat. With a brief look at me, she left the train.

By the time I'd got off, gone through the small ticket booth, and begun to walk up the lane home, she was standing there waiting for me.

I don't know why I should have felt so surprised. She'd crawled under the seat in front of me, I was the only one who knew she was there, and I'd kept her secret, so it would seem natural for her to trust me. But what on earth was I supposed to do with her?

All the way back to the cottage, I tried to engage the girl in conversation, but she remained as silent as she had been on the train. I didn't even know her name. Glancing at my watch, I noted it was a quarter past seven. We'd probably be home by half past and I'd get her some food and a warm drink and then make up the spare room for her.

There was still no sign of Phantom and I wondered if he would be at the cottage by the time we got there.

Fifteen minutes later we arrived home. It was cold so I put a match to the fire that I'd laid that morning and set about things in the kitchen whilst it slowly infused the room with warmth.

Placing hot milk, toast, jam, and a few biscuits on the table for the child I went upstairs to make her bed.

On my return I found the empty dishes in a pile on the draining board and the girl crouched on the floor in front of the fire.

I took my tea and sat in a chair next to her. I'd tried to put my arm around her shoulders on the walk home, but she'd immediately shied away. I wanted to offer her some sort of physical comfort—she was so obviously lacking in affection—but, by the same token I didn't want to frighten her. I supposed I'd just have to be patient and let her go at her own pace.

"You know I don't even know your name," I said. She looked up at me with huge brown eyes, but still said nothing and then turned back to gaze at the flames.

"Well, I can't very well call you child. I'll call you Poppy for now if that's all right with you, just until you're ready to tell me your real name?"

At that she nodded briefly then rose and stood at the foot of the stairs, apparently it was time for bed.

As I stood to accompany her, Phantom appeared.

"Oh, so you've decided to come home, have you?" I said. At that Poppy turned and looked at me. I'd forgotten once again to keep my mouth shut, and was about to open it again to explain when to my utter amazement she reached down, scooped Phantom up in a hug and carried him upstairs. And Phantom was quite happy to let her do so.

As I entered the bedroom I found Poppy already fast asleep in bed, her shoes set neatly at the foot and her coat folded on the chair. Phantom was also asleep, curled up on the eiderdown with Poppy's arm hugging him close.

So I wasn't the only one who could see this ghost cat. I'd heard tell that children were more open to these sorts of encounters with imaginary friends and suchlike, but I was a little perturbed. For some reason I couldn't help but feel there was more to this encounter than met the eye, and what I initially thought of as coincidence wasn't one at all.

CHAPTER FIVE

Monday morning came bright and early, and as I opened the curtains I was greeted with sunshine and a pale blue sky. It promised to be a glorious autumn day and I wondered whether I should continue unpacking inside the house or venture out into the garden. Or even take a walk along the beach. Then I remembered!

Grabbing my dressing gown, I hurriedly put it on whilst dashing to the spare room down the hall. It was empty and the bed made up neatly. Had I dreamed it all?

Scrambling downstairs in a most unladylike manner, I was relieved to see both Poppy and Phantom curled up together in a chair.

"Good morning," I said cheerfully as I made my way to the kitchen.

"I hope you slept well, Poppy. I'll make you some breakfast and then I thought perhaps you'd like to go and play in the garden. The front is quite safe and has lots of magical things to find if you look closely enough."

As I set to scrambling eggs and making toast, Poppy wandered out to the front with Phantom on her heels and sat on the stoop. I could see her looking around the flowerbeds to see what I meant by magical things; then suddenly she spied something and off they went.

I'll never forget the first time I had seen the cottage garden. I was a little older than Poppy and had peered over the gate drawn to the promises beyond the high hedge.

It was like a fairytale with all the flowers in bloom, and I'd made up stories as to whom it could possibly have belonged. I rather fancied the idea of Cinderella living there with her stepmother and sisters. Or Hansel and Gretel after they'd escaped from the wicked witch. I'd spied several things that day under the foliage: a ring of toad-stools, a giant's boot and a huge dragonfly nestling in the apple tree.

I had of course added to the wonders in the garden myself since moving in. Several ornate butterflies, a family of frogs, and a num-ber of miniature houses were all carefully hidden unless you knew just where to look.

I stood at the window eating my toast as I watched Poppy and Phantom searching, and smiled when I saw the look of amazement on Poppy's face as she discovered the next wonder.

"Poppy, come in and eat your breakfast now, it's on the table for you." As she came in and seated herself I said, "I'm just going to dress. I'll be upstairs if you need me."

She looked at me and gave her usual brief nod but remained silent. I was beginning to wonder if she'd ever speak.

Once dressed, I went to Poppy's room and opened the curtains to let in the sunshine. Turning, I spied something stuck down the side of the chair cushion. It was a gentleman's wallet. It must have fallen out of Poppy's pocket when she'd taken her coat off last night.

I wondered what she was doing with a wallet. Could it belong to her—a gift from her father perhaps?

Well, I had to make sure, so I opened it and got the most awful shock. It belonged to Peter Clairmont! I sat on the chair whilst I contemplated what this could mean, but no matter how hard I tried I could only come up with one explanation: she had picked his pocket.

Opening it again, I saw there were various pieces of identification. These all showed that Peter was obviously the owner, but there was also a tidy sum of money in it. So whilst Poppy had stolen his wallet, she hadn't removed the money and thrown away the incriminating evidence, which is what I would have expected a thief to do. The more I thought about it the less sense it made. There really was nothing left to do except to go down and confront her.

I found her still sitting quietly at the table. Her food was gone and the crockery once again was stacked on the draining board.

I took the seat opposite her and then slowly pulled the wallet from my pocket, laying it on the table between us. She looked at it, then at me and smiled. Of all the things she could have done—run from the house, burst into tears, snatched the wallet back—that she would smile never crossed my mind, but what did it mean? Did she want me to find it?

"Poppy, did you steal this wallet yesterday at the train station?"

A shake of the head, no.

"Well, was it given to you?"

Another no. I sighed, trying to extract information like this was wearying but I had to know the truth.

"Do you know the person it belongs to?"

A nod, yes. We were starting to get somewhere.

"Did you find it?"

Another nod.

"At the station yesterday?"

No.

I thought for a moment, trying to work out the next question. "Well, did someone else steal it and perhaps drop it and then you found it?"

No.

I couldn't think what else to ask. None of it made sense. She hadn't stolen the wallet, it wasn't given to her, she knew who it belonged to and had found it, but not at the train station yesterday when I knew for certain Peter had been there and when Poppy came rushing into the carriage as though the very devil were on her heels. Obviously with the wallet in her coat pocket, otherwise it wouldn't have been on the chair this morning.

"Poppy, you do realise that I also know the owner of this wallet, don't you?"

Yes, she nodded.

"And that I must return it to him?"

At this she nodded enthusiastically and grinned. I was completely confounded. It was as though this was what she was waiting for me to say—that I had every intention of returning it. But what could it mean?

"All right. Well, I'm afraid I can't leave you here alone. You'll have to accompany me back to London and I'll return the wallet to Mr. Clairmont."

I stood and went to the phone with the intention of calling Jerry to obtain Peter's number. As I lifted the phone to dial, Phantom shot out of nowhere and batted the receiver from my hand.

"Phantom, for goodness sake, what on earth has got into you?" I glanced over at Poppy as she walked to the phone and returned the receiver to its cradle, and then shook her head.

"You don't want me to contact Mr. Clairmont?" I asked. "You want me to just turn up unannounced and hope he's at the orphanage?"

Poppy nodded solemnly. It was obviously important to her that I do it her way. She'd made no secret of the wallet particularly and she was both understanding and accepting that I had to return it. She was also prepared to accompany me. I looked at Phantom, who sat on his haunches next to Poppy with a patient look on his face. I was definitely outnumbered.

"Fine, I'll do as you ask although I don't understand it." Grabbing my bag coat and keys I said, "Come on then, if we get a move on we'll make the ten-fifteen."

Thank goodness, I thought later, that I had no idea what I was about to discover as I hurried down the lane with a small child skipping beside me and a ghost cat leading the way.

CHAPTER SIX

A s I began to climb the orphanage steps I glanced back at Poppy, who had stopped at the bottom and was clinging to the rail. She obviously wasn't prepared to go any further. I nodded to let her know I understood and, looking back, I couldn't say I blamed her. The building was a Gothic horror. Overwhelmingly huge with towering parapets and monstrous-faced gargoyles.

Large as it was, it blocked out all the light and left the area in dark foreboding shadows. Soot-blackened bricks gave it a menacing aura and small grimy windows, that I doubted had ever been cleaned, gazed out like sightless eyes.

Taking a deep breath, I made my way inside and was greeted by a woman in uniform whom I assumed was the Matron.

"Can I help you?" she asked.

"Yes, I'm here to see Mr. Clairmont. Is he available?"

"Do you have an appointment?"

"No, I'm afraid I don't, but if it's not convenient I'd be happy to call another time."

"I'm sure that won't be necessary. He's in a meeting at the moment but I'll let him know you're here. You can wait in there," she said, pointing to an open door behind me. "He shouldn't be much longer."

"Thank you," I said and made my way to the indicated room.

It was as dispiriting in here as it was outside. Dark wood paneling on the walls rose from floor to ceiling of the cavernous space, and although there were a number of table lamps lit they couldn't compete with the gloomy decor and barely made a difference.

The rugs on the blackened floor were dull, dusty and frayed, as were the covers and cushions on the meagre supply of chairs. Works of art adorned the walls but again were filthy and the subject matter either thoroughly depressing, like the seascapes and landscapes, or positively frightening, like several of the portraits and the religious scenes, which seemed to focus on the hellfire and damnation aspects of religion.

I shuddered involuntarily, how could any child survive in surroundings as bleak and joyless as these? It seemed to me that no matter how much fund-raising was done, the task to bring warmth, love, light and happiness into this place was nigh on impossible.

At the end of the room was a large built-in bookcase with glass-fronted doors and internal lights and as I moved closer, I realised it was a display of some kind.

Various photographs adorned the shelving, along with more personal items like books and dried flowers, and in one instance a tortoiseshell comb. At first I couldn't work out what it meant, but as I studied some of the photographs, and saw a small sign of remembrance for those that had been lost, it dawned on me what I was looking at. I was so stunned that I didn't hear the footsteps behind me and nearly jumped out of my skin when a voice spoke.

"Ella! What a lovely surprise. I didn't expect to see you again so soon." It was Peter.

I turned to face him and forced myself to smile. "Oh yes, well neither did I. Actually I'm sorry to have turned up unannounced."

"Oh, it's no trouble at all. It was a good excuse to leave a thoroughly boring meeting."

I nodded, then looked back at the display. Peter obviously saw the look of distress on my face and moved closer.

"I'm sorry you had to see this alone," he began. "But we feel it's appropriate to remember them in this small way. It was my idea actually."

"I understand, of course. It was just a shock when I realised what it was. Can you tell me about them, how they died?"

There were at least two dozen photographs, all of them children who had resided at the orphanage at one time or another, and all who had met their deaths far too early. They'd barely had time to live and what life they'd had must have been so difficult and lonely.

"Well, some of them were before my time, of course, but I'll tell you what I can." Pointing at one of the images he said, "This was Cedric. He contracted pneumonia and after a short illness passed away in his sleep. He was six years old."

I looked at the photograph of a tiny, under-nourished looking boy in a too-large jacket and a cap. He had an adorable cheeky face and a gap-toothed smile. I doubted the tooth fairy had ever visited him.

"This was Elizabeth. She was a little older than Cedric at nine. She ran into the road and startled a horse and carriage. The horse reared and brought his hooves down on her head. She died instantly. There was nothing anyone could do, it happened so fast." Another beautiful innocent child smiled back at me from the grainy black and white portrait.

As we moved up the display Peter stopped in front of a photograph of a beautiful dark-haired girl. "This was Mary. She was the one I told you about."

"The one that drowned?"

He nodded and I noticed him grit his teeth and clench his hands into fists. "She was only twelve."

I'd moved up almost to the end and was looking at another young girl. "And this one?"

"That was Millicent. She was only seven."

"What happened to her?"

"She slipped and fell in front of an oncoming train."

I gasped. "Oh, how awful. Was it recently?"

"Well, more recent than the others, but it was over a year ago. Why do you ask?" He said with a frown.

Just as I was about to answer, the Matron came in with a box and interrupted us. "A lady just dropped these donations off, Mr. Clairmont. Where would you like them?"

"Just put them in my office for now, Matron, thank you."

"I'm sorry, you must be busy," I said. "I'll leave you to get on with your work."

As I started to leave the room, Peter called after me.

"Ella, was there something in particular you came to see me about?"

Oh, I'd forgotten all about the reason for my being there in the first place! Luckily, the Matron's previous interruption had planted a much-welcomed seed in my mind. I turned, and for an instant swore I saw a look of disdain on his face, but then it disappeared to be replaced by a smile. I must have imagined it.

"Of course there was. It completely slipped my mind. As you know, I've moved recently and I've now far too many belongings. I wondered if you'd like me to donate them to the orphanage."

"Well, that would be very kind of you, Ella. We can always use more donations, thank you. Did you come all this way to ask me that?"

I smiled. "It wasn't a special journey, if that's what you mean. I had to come up to the city for an appointment, so it seemed prudent to pop in and ask at the same time."

He nodded. "Well, that explains it."

"I must dash if I'm to catch my train home. It was nice to see you again, Peter. I'll get those donations packed up soon. Bye for now," I said as I turned on my heel and waved over my shoulder. I forced myself not to run but it was a challenge, I just wanted to get away from the horrible place.

By the time I'd reached the bottom of the steps I found Poppy was nowhere in sight, I could only hope she wasn't too far away and would see me leaving. Glancing back, I saw Peter staring at me from the doorway, but this time the look on his face was unreadable.

CHAPTER SEVEN

As I dashed through central London in my eagerness to get as far away as possible from Peter Clairmont and the orphanage, I literally ran smack into a woman coming the other way.

"I'm terribly sorry, I wasn't looking where ... Oh, Ginny, it's you. Thank goodness."

"Ella! Heavens above, what's happened? Is someone chasing you?"

"No, nothing like that. I was just in a rush to get to the station before I missed my train."

"Darling, I have to say you're not looking at all well. In fact you look like you've just seen a ghost. Are you all right?"

I burst out laughing, I couldn't help it. *'Seen a ghost!'* If only she knew.

"Well, that settles it," Ginny announced. "You're obviously hysterical, something must have happened. I insist you come home with me and have a cup of tea, or possibly something stronger. Then you can tell me all about it." And with that she linked arms and steered me towards the apartment.

As we rounded the corner I happened to glance at the small park that sat opposite Jerry and Ginny's building. Sitting on one of the seats was Poppy, with Phantom next to her. Oh, thank goodness. She waved and indicated that she would wait for me there. I thought that would be for the best under the circumstances, so after a quick nod I followed Ginny into the foyer.

In the apartment Ginny divested me of my coat, hat, gloves and bag, then proceeded to the kitchen to ask the maid to make some tea.

In the drawing room she poured us each a small sherry and then, making herself comfortable in an armchair, she asked what on earth was going on.

"Oh, Ginny, I don't know where to start," I confessed.

"Well, I always find the beginning is as good a place as any. Of course, if you want to begin by telling me why you were racing down the high street as though being chased by a pack of hell hounds, be my guest."

"Actually I'd just come from meeting Peter Clairmont at the orphanage."

"Oh, Ella! He didn't molest you or anything awful, did he?" she asked, shocked.

"No, Ginny he did not, and please don't jump to conclusions like that. I went to return something to him but had second thoughts. Actually that reminds me, do you have any spare clothing, books or children's games, or perhaps bedding? You know, things you no longer need?"

"What? Ella darling, you're not making any sense. Here, have some more sherry. Now what do you mean do I have bedding or games? I say, are you planning a slumber party with Peter Clairmont? How wicked, Ella!" she said, laughing.

"Ginny, really, of course not. I idiotically happened to mention that I had some unwanted items to donate to the orphanage, but the fact is, I haven't. Of course, I can't let Peter know that otherwise he'll think I was there for some other reason altogether. Which of course I was, but I can't let him know that, otherwise he'll know I'm onto him, don't you see?"

"Not really, no. Could you explain?"

As I was trying to gather my thoughts into a more cohesive pattern the maid came in with the tea. Pouring, Ginny said, "I think it would be better if you started at the beginning, Ella. I can't make any sense at all of what you've said so far, darling."

I took a deep breath. "Ginny, do you believe in ghosts?"

"Oh, I see, this is about your cat?"

"What?"

"Your cat. You know, the black apparition that came to lunch with you yesterday."

I was astonished. "You mean you could see him?"

"Well, I certainly saw him sitting in the kitchen chair, and I knew he was the one who caused you to spill your coffee."

"Why didn't you say anything?"

"Dearest, when exactly have I had time? I could hardly say anything at lunch lest both our guest and Jerry thought we'd gone mad."

She did have a point I supposed. It seemed much longer considering all that had happened to me, but it was actually less than twenty-four hours.

"Do you have some sort of special gift, Ginny, and does Jerry know?"

"Sadly I have no particular gift. It happens very rarely and usually when I'm in the company of an adept such as yourself. It's a legacy from one of my Romanian ancestors."

"Really? How fascinating. I didn't know your history was filled with such colour," I said in awe.

"Heavens, that's just one branch darling. I'm fairly sure one of my great-great-grandmothers on the maternal side was burned at the stake. It's a wonder I'm here at all."

"And is Jerry aware?"

"Of course he is. Jerry and I have no secrets. But because it's such a rare occurrence it's not something we've discussed in detail. But never mind me. We need to talk about your sudden ability. It is something that has only happened recently, correct?"

I nodded. "Yes, it all started when I went to view the cottage for the first time."

"How interesting. Start again and tell me everything." And so I started at the beginning, when I felt as though I'd been steered by an unseen hand to discover the agent who was selling The Yellow Cottage.

By the time I'd got to the part where Poppy had rushed into the carriage and scrambled under the seat facing mine, Ginny was in raptures.

"Good heavens, Ella. What happened to her?"

"She fell asleep until it was my stop, then she got off and was waiting for me halfway up the lane. What else could I do but take her home?"

"So where is she now, back at the cottage?" Ginny asked.

"Good heavens, no. I couldn't leave her there alone. I brought her with me. She's waiting for me in the park across the road."

Ginny stood up. "We can't leave the poor girl there. I'll go and bring her in."

"No, Ginny, honestly it's fine. She really didn't want to come in. She's not spoken a word yet and I don't want to overwhelm her." I rose and went to the window overlooking the park. "It's all right," I said, giving a small wave. "She's still there."

"Well, of course, Ella, whatever you think is best. So, what happened next? Why did you go to the orphanage?"

"Oh, yes. Well, when I went into Poppy's room this morning, I found a gentleman's wallet on the chair. I thought it strange so I opened it, and guess who it belonged to."

Ginny shook her head. "I've no idea, who?"

"Peter Clairmont."

"No!" she exclaimed. "How extraordinary. How did she get it?"

"Well, I thought she must have picked his pocket at the station last night, but now I know that's impossible. It…"

"Darling, I'm home. Where are you?"

It was Jerry.

"In the drawing room, Jerry."

Jerry walked in. "Hello, Ella, I didn't expect to see you here. Guess who I bumped into on the way home?"

I glanced up just as Jerry said "Peter," to see the man himself walk in. Oh no, how much had he heard?

"Ella, what a surprise. I thought you were rushing to catch your train," he said as he came and sat in the chair next to me. It may have been my imagination but I could have sworn he made that sound like an accusation.

I'd frozen. For some reason I couldn't think of a single thing to say. Luckily Ginny, cool and calm as always, answered for me.

"Oh, she was. I bumped into her as she'd almost got to the station but insisted she come home with me. We so rarely get girl-time together and it was a perfect opportunity to catch up properly. We've had a lovely afternoon discussing the cottage and the island. In fact, I've decided I'm going to go back with Ella this evening to spend a few days down there. I think the sea air will do me a world of good. That's if you don't mind, Jerry?"

"Of course I don't, darling. You go and have some fun. I'll be perfectly all right. I'm working on my new manuscript anyway. No, I think it's a wonderful idea. When were you thinking of going? It's five now," he said, glancing at his watch.

"We were just waiting for you actually. We thought the six o'clock if you were back in time and could drop us off. I do so hate dragging my luggage down the street."

Jerry laughed. "Of course I'll have the car brought round. Peter, I shan't be long, old boy. You're more than welcome to join us, or you can stay here if you'd prefer?"

"Thank you, Jerry, that's very kind I must say. Yes, I'll wait for you here. Perhaps I could have a look at some of your books whilst I wait?"

"Certainly. I'll show you through to the library and if you need anything just ask the staff. I won't be long."

Ginny and I briefly caught the other's eye. I was concerned that Jerry was getting too friendly with Peter. I would have to warn him somehow without giving the game away.

Ginny turned and said, "It's very nice to see you again, Peter, but if you'll excuse us, I need Ella to help me choose some suitable attire for life on the island."

I almost rolled my eyes. It was an hour's train journey away, not Antarctica. Heaven knows what she was planning on packing. I hurriedly said goodbye to Peter and Ginny took my arm, almost dragging me down the hall.

"For goodness sake, Ginny." I whispered, suppressing a smile. "Don't you think you're going a bit overboard? He'll smell a rat for sure if you keep this up."

"Nonsense. Men are clueless when faced with either beauty, or damsels in distress. He won't suspect a thing."

Whilst I understood her reasoning—in fact I had seen her womanly wiles in action to great effect on a number of occasions—I wasn't so sure it would wash with Peter Clairmont. There was something about him that just didn't ring true and I was determined to find out what it was.

CHAPTER EIGHT

As Ginny and I were settling into our carriage for the journey home, I spied Poppy entering one of the others. She obviously didn't want to be seen, but I was extremely relieved to know she was there.

Ginny and I had barely had a chance to discuss that day's events, and as the train was full to the gills we decided to wait until we got home.

Back on the island, Ginny flagged down a taxi. She really *didn't* like dragging her luggage, and looking at the amount she'd decided to bring, it would have been impossible for just the two of us anyway.

I'm not sure how long she was planning to stay, but I thought four hat-boxes, three suitcases, and a carry-on a little extravagant. But that was Ginny to a T and I couldn't help but love her for it. I must admit the motor car was a pleasant change from walking, although I did miss the scenery along the coastal path.

Half an hour later, we were warm and cosy in the cottage and I was just waiting for the kettle to boil when I spied Poppy in the garden. She was obviously waiting to enter but not prepared to do so whilst Ginny was there. I had to think of an excuse to get Ginny out of the room in order for her to sneak in.

Whilst I was contemplating what to say, Ginny in an uncanny act of prescience said, "Well, are you going to give me the tour, darling? I love what I've seen so far."

"Of course, we can start with your room and take your luggage up too," I said.

Staggering up the stairs under the weight of Ginny's belongings, I noticed Phantom sitting in the hall. I guessed that meant Poppy wasn't far behind. Entering the largest of the four bedrooms I said to Ginny, "I thought you'd like this room the best. It's the largest and the one with the most closet space."

"Oh, you know me so well, Ella dear. I must say it is rather beautiful." And it was. I had barely done anything to the decor myself; just put a few knick-knacks around the place, but it was very grand. The four-poster bed with its lemon yellow floral canopy and eiderdown, lent a cheery ambience to the room, and the fabric had been mirrored in the other soft furnishings. The chaise longue at the foot of the bed was done in deep green velvet, as was the stool at the dressing table. But my absolute favourites were the small chandelier with its tear-drop crystals and the matching lamps on either side of the bed.

"Thank you, Ginny, plus it has a wonderful view of the back garden all the way down to the river. Now I'm afraid I'll have to leave you to unpack. I haven't had chance to find a daily as yet."

"There's no need to worry about that, Ella dear. I'm used to roughing it a little sometimes, you know. And I want no argument from you but I insist on helping you with your unpacking. Now come along and let's finish our tea and you can tell me what happened today. I'll have a look around the rest of the place in the daylight."

We made our way back downstairs, but not before I took a chance to check in on Poppy. She was fast asleep in her room with Phantom by her side.

Once again settled in front of the fire, I said, "Now, how far had I got Ginny?"

"You were just about to tell me about the wallet."

"Oh, yes. Well, first I need to go back a little bit. You see when I got to the orphanage, the matron showed me to a waiting room, a huge dark and dismal place with barely any light, but at one end there was a display cabinet and inside were around twenty or so black and white photographs of children, along with books and dried flowers and other keepsakes. At first I couldn't work out what it was, but then I realised it was a sort of shrine."

"A shrine... whatever do you mean?"

"It was a way of remembering all the former orphans who had died whilst living there."

"Oh, Ella, how terribly sad."

"I know, isn't it? Then Peter came in and saw me looking. It was his idea apparently to remember them all in that way. But that's not all. I asked him to tell me how they had died."

"Heavens, Ella, don't you think that was a little... macabre?" asked Ginny.

"It was a gut feeling, Ginny. I just felt I needed to know for some reason. Anyway he proceeded to tell me about several of the children. One died of pneumonia, a little boy aged just six, another was killed by a rearing horse when she ran out into the road, and Mary—Peter had already told me about her when he walked me to the station on Sunday evening—she was drowned on an outing to this very island, Ginny. Peter was there at the time too. It was when he was living at the orphanage for that short time."

"It's all so very heartbreaking, isn't it, Ella? So is that when you told him about the wallet?"

"Oh, no, he doesn't know I have it. I'd obviously gone there to return it but you see he gave himself away when he was telling me about the children. That's why I made up that nonsense about the donations."

Ginny frowned. "But how did he give himself away? He didn't have anything to do with those three deaths, did he?"

"Not those three, no, but he told me about a fourth, a seven-year-old girl named Millicent. She died at a train station, Ginny. She fell on to the track seconds before the train pulled in."

Ginny covered her mouth and widened her eyes in shock. "You don't mean … ?"

I nodded. "Yes, I do. Poppy, the girl who came home with me, is Millicent, and she died over a year ago."

"Oh, I say! That means Peter must have been there at the time, otherwise how would Poppy, I mean Milly, have got hold of the wallet?"

"Exactly, Ginny. So you see now why I couldn't return it to Peter."

"Yes, I do, Ella. But whatever are we going to do now? Peter must be involved in the death of that child in some way, would you agree?"

I nodded. "He must have been. Whether it was a tragic accident like he said or something altogether more sinister, he was definitely there. Why else would Milly come to me? I think it must have happened at that train station. It fact, it could have been that very train, at that very time, just a year prior. I think it was Phantom that led her to me and now I must solve the case in order for her to find peace."

"Well, thank heavens we warned Jerry not to get too close," said Ginny.

"I say, do you think Peter had anything to do with the girl that drowned?" she asked.

I thought about it. "I'm not sure, Ginny. I do hope not. He did seem genuinely upset when he spoke about it." I frowned as something else dawned on me. "More than the others actually, and he was angry."

"Well, perhaps they were related in some way. Cousins, or brother and sister, perhaps?"

I stared at her. "Why, Ginny, I do believe you may be onto something."

CHAPTER NINE

There was nothing more we could do that night, so Ginny and I went to bed, having decided to sleep on what we knew so far and make plans the next day.

Rising early, I was in the kitchen preparing a light breakfast for the two of us whilst waiting for Ginny to wake up. There was no longer any need to prepare something for Milly, not now I knew who she was.

I should have seen it sooner. I'd fixed food for her but had never actually seen her eat and the dishes were empty and stacked on the draining board each time, I just assumed she'd eaten it.

I shook my head, thinking how easily we take things at face value. Believing what we see as opposed to delving a little deeper for the truth, rather like seeing a magician's trick. We know the lady isn't really sawed in half but accept that she is, and then watch as she is miraculously made whole again. It's just a trick of the eye, a sleight of hand, smoke and mirrors. *Probably because we want to believe,* I thought. Or more to the point because we don't want to believe the alternative.

"Good morning, Ella, what a marvellous night's sleep I had. That room is absolutely divine. And the peace! So much different to waking up to noisy London traffic," Ginny said, coming down the stairs at a light trot.

I smiled and handed her a cup of tea. She looked absolutely impeccable as usual in grey wool and cream cashmere. I on the other hand was in my drab working clothes. I couldn't see the point in getting dressed up to unpack boxes. But perhaps Ginny had something else in mind.

As we took our seats at the breakfast table she said, "I've had an idea, Ella, about how we can solve this case of yours. I think we need to get a confession of some sort out of Peter Clairmont. We need to know for sure the depth of his involvement before we start making accusations."

"Oh, I agree, Ginny, I was thinking the same thing actually, but how do you suppose we go about it?"

"Well, I think we need to get the police commissioner involved."

"Oh, Ginny, really!" I exclaimed. "Why on earth would the commissioner be interested in what we have to say? Especially as we have no real evidence at this point and only a ghost child and a phantom cat as witnesses." Goodness, it sounded even more ridiculous when I said it out loud.

"Because, dearest, Uncle Albert will do anything for his only god-daughter," Ginny said with a wink.

After breakfast, whilst I washed up the dishes, Ginny made a telephone call to her godfather. I had no idea what she told him but she bounced back into the kitchen with a look of glee.

"Well, that's settled, Uncle Albert will be here at two so shall we crack on with those boxes of yours whilst we're waiting?"

I must give Ginny her due. She certainly knew how to crack the whip and get things in motion.

An exhausting four and a half hours later the boxes were unpacked and everything assigned a home, although not all put away, but it was lovely to be able to see the floor again. As I pottered about making some lunch, Ginny went upstairs to change. I supposed I should do the same considering the importance of our guest. Plus of course I wanted to appear as credible as possible. I still didn't know what we were going to tell him but I'm sure Ginny would have a plan as she usually did.

At two-o'-clock on the dot I heard the gate creak and Ginny went to the door to greet our guest. I hadn't realised Sir Albert Montesford was the Police Commissioner now. I'd met him very briefly when Jerry and Ginny had married but we hadn't really spoken at length. However, I recognised him as he waddled up the path and enfolded Ginny in a huge hug. He was quite easily the largest man I had ever seen.

As they came inside I offered my hand to shake, but to my amazement he waved it away and instead engulfed me in a hug as big as the one he'd given Ginny. "Isobella, it's lovely to see you again, my dear. Now what's all this about you seeing murdered ghosts?"

I sighed. Well, there went my idea to introduce the concept gently. The clever plan I assumed Ginny had hatched was obviously to tell him everything at once, no matter how ludicrous it sounded. I couldn't begin to fathom whether or not he believed a word of it, but he was here and prepared to listen, which was a start. Now we just had to convince him.

I decided something a little stronger than tea was needed, so as we moved into the drawing room I went to the drinks cabinet and poured us all a snifter of whiskey. As I was arranging the glasses and decanter on the tray I saw Milly and Phantom descend the stairs.

Once we were all seated Albert spoke. "Now before we get to discussing the case in more detail you both need to understand something. No doubt Ginny has told you how I am wrapped around her little finger," he said, looking at me with a twinkle in his eye.

I smiled thinking, *yes, something like that.*

Albert continued, "Of course to some extent that is perfectly true, however first and foremost I am a policeman and a former solicitor. I deal in tangible truths and evidence; things I can see with my own eyes and prove exist within the scope of the law."

Oh, dear, my heart was sinking with each word he spoke.

"That said, I know you, Isobella dear, we are practically family after all, and as Ginny so rightly pointed out on the telephone, you are level-headed and not one for hysterics. To that end I am here and prepared to listen to your story objectively." He paused.

"But?" Ginny asked.

Albert nodded. "But I would like to see some evidence of the girl. A demonstration of some kind perhaps?"

I had no idea whether Milly would be able, let alone agreeable to, providing a demonstration. I glanced over at her questioningly. She sat chewing her lip. Then, after what I could only assume was a signal from Phantom, nodded her head.

"Yes, I think that would be possible." I said. "Although, you must understand I have never asked her to do such a thing before and I can't guarantee what will happen, if it works at all."

"Is she in the room with us now?" Albert asked.

"Yes, she is," I said, but omitted mentioning she was sitting beside him.

"Very well, let's begin. Do we need to close the curtains and dim the lights?" he asked, perfectly seriously.

Ginny burst into peals of laughter. "Oh, Albert really, that nonsense is for charlatans and crooks. Ella is the genuine article, aren't you, darling?" she said, patting my hand. "There's really no need for theatrics. So what did you have in mind in order to convince you?"

Albert thought for a moment, then said, "Well, moving an object would seem to be the best solution. Perhaps the candelabra on the mantelshelf there? Would that be possible?"

I glanced above the fireplace. The candelabrum was solid silver and although it was heavy I felt sure Milly could lift it. However, there was a more immediate problem. She was too short to reach.

I was just about to voice my concern when Phantom nimbly leapt upon the shelf and swatted it with his paw. Such was the force of his swing that it flew through the air, scattering the candles to the four corners, and came to rest with a resounding crash in the middle of the table. I was exceptionally glad at that moment that Albert had not chosen my grandmother's crystal vase.

"Good God!" he exclaimed, pale-faced. After a moment or two of silence he held out his empty glass in a slightly shaking hand and said, "Be a dear and fill it up, would you?"

After dutifully refilling his glass, I sat back and watched as he very carefully examined the candelabrum. He then rose to examine the mantelshelf. I assumed he was looking for springs or something that would indicate it was a gimmick.

Seated once again, he said, "Well, I must admit that was an extraordinary display and I can see no obvious trickery involved, but I would like to see more."

"Of course," I said. "What else would you like to see?"

"That book on the shelf behind you, the green one with the bookmark just peeking out, can she bring it to me?"

I watched as Milly rose and went to the book in question, then turned back to observe Albert's reaction. From his perspective it would look as though the book were floating through mid-air.

Closer and closer it came, wobbling slightly as Milly strained under its weight. It was rather a large tome. As she neared Albert, she held it out in front of his nose and moved it slowly from side to side. I nearly laughed at her cheeky antics, especially as Albert's eyes were practically crossed in an attempt to keep it in view. Then Milly raised it as high as she could and let go. It landed with a resounding thump in his lap.

He sat staring at it, mesmerized, his hands in the air. I could see he was more than a little shocked so I leaned over and moved it. Placing it on the table seemed to break the spell. "Albert, it's just a book, really."

Glancing at Ginny I saw the look of shock and concern on her face too. I know she believed wholeheartedly in Milly. She had also seen Phantom with her own eyes. But still, I supposed it was a different matter altogether seeing demonstrations such as these in broad daylight.

"Are you all right, Ginny?" I asked.

She nodded, her eyes still glued to the book. "Yes, I'm fine, Ella. It just makes it all seem so real, you know, seeing it like this. We really must help her."

I turned to Albert. "Have you seen enough, Albert?"

"Yes, I rather think I have," he said, reaching for his whiskey glass.

At that moment Phantom sprang up from the floor. In midair, for a split second, he materialised into his solid form for all to see, and then on the downward arc, he vanished.

I looked at Albert. "That was Phantom, my ghost cat," I said. Then I rose to get him a cloth to wipe the whiskey from his face.

CHAPTER TEN

A lbert decided to stay the night in order for us to formulate a plan. He'd already made some telephone calls to ask his men to find out as much as possible about one Peter Clairmont. He'd also called Jerry, and once he'd explained the situation had asked that he get the next train down so he could talk to him face-to-face about what he knew.

Now Ginny was upstairs making up a room, whilst I was in the kitchen preparing dinner.

Shortly before six Jerry walked in, shaking out his umbrella and removing his sodden top-coat. I hadn't noticed but it had started to rain quite heavily.

"Why, Jerry, you're soaked! There's a fire lit in the drawing room. Go and get warm, and help yourself to a drink. Albert's already in there. He can tell you about today's events," I said.

"Thank you, Ella." He looked round appreciatively. "I must say I can see why you fell in love with this place, although it's certainly bigger than you led me to believe." He bent and gave me a quick kiss on the cheek. "You should have told me about the ghosts, you know. I would have understood."

"But would you have believed me? They're two quite different things."

He shrugged. "I most probably would have wanted proof like Albert. Perhaps you could organise that for later, do you think? I must say I'm rather intrigued."

"Well … I can't promise anything. I'd have to ask Milly. She's not a performing monkey, you know." Although Phantom was another story entirely, I thought. That last display surprised even me.

"I'll see what I can do. Now run along and get dry, and keep Albert company. He won't admit it but I think he's had rather a shock today."

As I was getting the roast out of the oven, I heard Albert say, "Jerry, good to see you, old boy. Thanks for coming down at such short notice. Got ourselves a bit of a mystery here which I'm hoping you can help with. I thought we'd discuss it properly with the girls over dinner. By the way, I got that latest book of yours. Fabulous stuff, and I didn't see the woman being the murderer."

"Well, that's a terrific compliment coming from the Police Commissioner, I must say," replied Jerry.

At that moment Ginny came waltzing down the stairs in yet another outfit and went to greet Jerry. "Darling, how good of you to come. It's so lovely to see you. And what do you think of the cottage? Marvellous, isn't it? Wait until you see our room, it's simply glorious. Now if you boys would deal with the wine, I'll help Ella with the food." A second later I heard the telephone ring and Ginny call out, "Albert, it's for you." I assumed that meant there was some news.

Once we were all seated Albert got straight to the point.

"That was Detective Inspector Wilkes on the phone and he's found out a very interesting little tidbit about our Mr. Clairmont. But before I tell you more I'd like to hear what Jerry knows."

"Well, to be honest," Jerry began, "I think I know the least of all of us. However, I'll tell you what I can. Ginny, could you pass the salt, please, darling?"

Just as Ginny stretched out her hand the saltcellar rose from the table and travelled through the air before depositing itself in front of him.

Jerry shot up like a bullet from a gun, knocking his chair over in the process. "Bloody Hell!" he swore, backing away from the table.

"Yes, that was my reaction too," intoned Albert, glaring in disgust at the faint whiskey stains still visible down his shirt.

"So that was Milly?" Jerry asked, looking at me.

"Yes. I haven't quite perfected the art of levitating objects myself yet."

"You can sit down again now, Jerry, your dinner is getting cold," said Ginny. As if on cue, which of course it was, Jerry's chair rose and sat itself upright in front of the table once again. Then Milly went to sit on the window seat. The demonstration was over.

"It's all right, Jerry, you can sit. That was the demonstration you asked for. There'll be no more," I said.

He slowly moved back to the table and tentatively sat down.

"Well, I never," he said, shaking his head. "I don't suppose I really believed until I saw that."

"That's how I felt, darling," said Ginny. "Now we really must help poor Milly find peace. Let's not forget she's the reason we're all here. Tell us what you know about Peter."

Jerry nodded. "As you know, it was at the orphanage fundraiser where I first met him. You had a prior engagement so couldn't attend with me, if you remember? Well, he kind of latched onto me, said he was a fan of my books."

"And you believed him?" asked Albert.

"Well, yes. To be honest, there was no doubt in my mind. We discussed at length two or three of my books and made reference to more; it was obvious he'd read them. Then we went on to discuss his own writing."

"He's a writer, you say?" Albert said, making notes in a little black book.

"Well, he said he was although he has yet to publish anything."

"Yes, he said that at lunch on Sunday, didn't he?" Ginny said. "Historical novels, wasn't it?"

"That's right. He said at the fundraiser that he had one manuscript almost completed, set in Ireland, I believe."

"He told me that too when he walked me to the station," I said, nodding. "He went to live in Ireland after leaving the orphanage. Apparently he had an aunt and uncle on his mother's side and he was sent to live with them after his parent's death," I said.

"Did he say anything else to you, Ella?" asked Albert, pen poised at the ready.

I paused, thinking back. "He said that he was nine when his parents died and that he was at the orphanage for around four months whilst his next of kin were being traced. He also mentioned day-trips the children took, down here actually. He came a couple of times but the last time one of the girls drowned. The trips stopped after that."

"How did he seem to you when he relayed that incident?"

"Certainly upset. He did say that was the reason he worked for the orphanage, to help raise the money to employ qualified staff.

He's of the opinion that had there been someone there that day who was trained, the girl could have been saved."

Albert was nodding and making notes.

"Ella and I wondered if the girl could have been his sister," said Ginny.

"And why would you think that?" asked Albert.

"He pointed out her photograph to Ella and she thought he seemed … how did you put it, Ella?"

"He seemed to take it more personally. He was quite angry about Mary actually, more so than the others, but of course that could just be because he witnessed it. I said at the time how traumatic it must have been for him and the other children."

"Her name was Mary, you say?" Albert asked.

I nodded.

"No other names, I suppose?"

"No, he just said Mary. Although the orphanage will have the details, I expect. In fact it may be written in the display cabinet somewhere and I missed it."

"Do you think they could be related, Albert?" asked Jerry.

"It's possible. I'll have one of my men find out her full name and details surreptitiously. We don't want to tip our hand too soon. However, she certainly won't be related to Peter Clairmont."

"Whatever do you mean, Albert? I thought you just said Peter and this girl could be related?" said an exasperated Ginny. I must admit I was thoroughly confused myself.

"Oh, the girl and our man could be related, but I'm afraid the real Peter Clairmont died in a suspicious house fire in Yorkshire some eighteen months ago."

"What?" we all exclaimed in unison.

"Oh, yes. DI Wilkes was adamant," Albert said.

"But how do you know it's the same man that our Peter Clairmont is impersonating?" Jerry asked.

"Because of the information left in the wallet that Ella found. It contained, amongst other things, a National Identity Card."

Of course, I remembered now. I'd seen it when I was first looking through the wallet. I'd not taken much notice of what it was at the time, I'd been too shocked to see Peter's name on it.

"Really? I thought those things were scrapped after the war," said Jerry.

"Exactly, Jerry. You've hit the nail on the head so to speak. Considering they were first introduced in 1915 and put to sleep in 1919, this would mean our man would be, at a minimum, thirty-two years of age."

"Well, I don't suppose that's outside the realms of possibility. Although I must admit he does look considerably younger," said Jerry.

"I agree," Ginny said, wrinkling her nose in protest. "He doesn't look a year over twenty-five, if you ask me, but that still doesn't prove anything, Albert."

"Not alone of course, however my man Wilkes did some extra digging. It turns out that the NIC number on the card was registered in 1916 to a Mr. Peter Clairmont, age thirty-four."

"Oh, I say, that would put him at fifty-three today then," said Jerry.

"Precisely," said Albert. "The same age as the deceased incidentally."

"I'd wager he's taken other documents then. I mean, *if* he's taken on the identity of this man, then it makes sense to go the whole hog, as it were and take the lot," said Jerry.

"Heavens, he probably took his money as well," exclaimed Ginny.

"Aren't we forgetting one vital piece of information?" I asked, looking at the faces before me. Jerry and Ginny waited but I could see Albert knew what I was going to say.

"If our Peter has taken this man's identity and goodness knows what else, then he must have killed him to do it. The Peter Clairmont we know is a murderer."

I glanced over at Milly who had been silently listening to our exchange. "But I think we knew that already," I said softly.

CHAPTER ELEVEN

"So what exactly are we proposing to do now?" asked Ginny as we settled in the drawing room with coffee. I glanced at the mantel clock and saw it was already nine-thirty. It was going to be a late night.

"Hmm, we obviously need to flush him out somehow," said Jerry. "Wouldn't you agree, Albert?"

"I would indeed, but it's paramount he doesn't suspect anything. I've already got a man on his tail to see where he goes and who he contacts, and I've dispatched another up to Yorkshire to see what he can discover up there. What we need, as a matter of some urgency, are the details of the drowned girl. I believe once we have that information we'll find out who this man really is."

"Do you have someone looking for information about Mary?" I asked.

"I do," Albert said. "However, I've told him to steer clear of the orphanage at present, just find out what he can from other sources.

If we go in there and start asking questions our man will smell a rat for sure, and if he runs we may never find him again."

I thought about that for a minute. I'd been ruminating over an idea ever since Albert had revealed that Peter Clairmont was actually a fraud. And not only a fraud, but a probable murderer too. I glanced once again at Milly and made up my mind.

"Well, of course I could go in there. He's already expecting me with the donations, remember?"

"Absolutely not, Ella," said Jerry immediately. "You'd be going straight into the lion's den. It's too dangerous."

"Jerry, he doesn't know that we're onto him," I said. "What would seem more suspicious is if I didn't go when I've already said I would."

"Oh, dear, Ella is right, Jerry. She's going to have to make good on that promise sooner or later," Ginny said.

Jerry got up and started to pace back and forth, running his hand through his hair. He was terribly worried, I could see that, but I also knew I was the only one who could get close enough to Peter to find out the truth.

"He told me he found me easy to talk to, Jerry. Now that may very well be a ruse but I have to take that chance."

"I don't like it, Ella. You'll be vulnerable and alone. I can't let you put yourself in harm's way like that."

"But I won't be alone, Jerry," I said. "I can hardly carry the boxes myself. I'll need assistance." Turning to Albert I asked, "Albert, do you have a man who could help? Someone who could be undercover to accompany me as a chauffeur and delivery boy?"

Albert stood. "Ella, I do believe you've hit on a way to get the information we need. And yes, I do have a man perfect for the job. However, I echo Jerry's concerns. This could be dangerous. If he suspects for even one minute why you are really there, it could turn nasty and we don't know what he will do if cornered."

"And we certainly know he's capable of murder," said Jerry.

Ginny leaned over and took my hand. "Ella, are you absolutely sure about this, darling? It doesn't have to be you, you know. I'm sure given a bit of time we could work out another plan."

"Honestly, I'll be fine. I'll have Albert's man with me, I'll be in the orphanage where there are other staff and children and I promise I won't do anything to put myself at risk."

I looked up at Jerry and Albert, then back at Ginny.

"So does that put everyone's mind at ease?"

Jerry finally sat back down and leaned back, saying, "The only thing that would put my mind at ease would be if you weren't going. But I can see yours is made up. However, I'd like some assurances from Albert that there will be someone other than his undercover chap looking out for you."

"Of course," said Albert. "That goes without saying. I'll post several of my men in the vicinity."

"Good," I said, standing and addressing them all. "I suggest that we do this as soon as possible. Ginny, I'll need your help with some donations. I have some items I can get together, but not nearly enough."

"I have more than enough, Ella. Jerry and I can go back tomorrow and sort out some items. All right, darling?"

"Yes, all right. I'll throw in a signed copy of my latest novel too. I doubt he has it, as it's only just been published."

"Jerry, that's an excellent idea," I said. "I'll say it's a gift for him personally from you. That should get him thinking we are all friends, and stop him suspecting anything."

"And I can have my men ready as soon as you give the word," confirmed Albert. "I'll send Jimmy, one of my best officers, with you as chauffeur. When did you have in mind?"

"How about the day after tomorrow? We should have everything boxed up by then," I said.

Everybody nodded.

"Right, well, Thursday it is then. Now if you don't mind, it's been rather a long day and I'd like to head up to bed."

Ginny rose too. "I think we'll all benefit from a good night's sleep actually. We have a busy day ahead of us tomorrow."

"Yes, and possibly a perilous one after that," Jerry warned.

It wasn't until much later that I remembered Jerry's words and realized just how much we'd all underestimated Peter Clairmont.

CHAPTER TWELVE

Even though we'd all gone to bed late the night before, the next morning found us all up, dressed, and having breakfast by six-thirty.

I for one had slept solidly for two or three hours, and then had found myself wide awake, at four am. I dozed on and off for a while, during which time my mind ran through everything we had planned, over and over in a never-ending loop. This had left me feeling groggy. Consequently, my head felt as though it were stuffed with cotton wool, and I could feel the onset of a headache.

Looking around the table, I could see that Ginny and Jerry were feeling the same. Albert, on the other hand, looked as he always did. I supposed it was because he was used to dealing with nasty business like this, whereas the rest of us were complete novices.

As he began to liberally spread his toast with butter, topping it off with strawberry preserve, he looked at me.

"Ella, how are you feeling about everything this morning? Still wanting to go ahead? I know how different things can seem in the cold light of day, and I want to make sure you're not taking on more than you can handle."

"I'm determined to see this through, Albert. I admit to being nervous, but I suspect that's perfectly normal considering the circumstances."

"I'd be more than happy to go in your place, Ella," Jerry said.

"I know that, Jerry, I really do, and I appreciate it. But I think he will be more open and forthcoming with a woman. All I'm going to do is to engage him in conversation and get Mary's full name. It's not as though I intend to go in and accuse him of murder. I can't see why he would suspect anything from that. Then I simply pass on what I've found out to Albert."

Jerry sighed. "Well, when you put it like that, I suppose it's simple enough. But promise you won't do anything foolhardy."

"I promise," I said. "Now, what are the plans for today?"

"I think the best thing is for us to help you pack up your donations here. Then we can all head back to London. I'd feel much happier if you stayed the night with Jerry and me. We can sort out what we intend to give this afternoon. Then we'll be ready in the morning. Does that work for you, Albert?" Ginny asked.

"Yes, that would work out particularly well. I motored down here, so I'll give you all a lift back then head to the yard and apprise DI Wilkes."

"I'll need to telephone Peter to let him know I'll be there tomorrow," I said. "I don't want to just turn up. We need to be sure he's not otherwise engaged. Jerry, do you have the telephone number?"

Jerry rooted through his wallet and brought out a card. "Here it is."

"I must say, I think you're awfully brave, Ella," said Ginny. "Even if poor Milly were an accidental murder, Peter is certainly guilty of doing away with the real Clairmont."

Jerry chuckled, and swapped an amused glance with Albert. "Ginny, there is no such thing as an accidental murder. It's either one or the other. I think the term you're looking for is manslaughter."

"Well, I think that's just splitting hairs, Jerry. The point I'm trying to make is that this chap is dangerous, and capable of doing the most awful things. To go and knowingly confront him, as Ella is doing, takes a lot of guts. And I admire her tremendously."

"Of course, you are right, Ginny. We all admire what Ella is doing," agreed Jerry.

Glancing at the clock, I noticed how early it still was. "I'll call at a more reasonable hour. In the meantime, Ginny and I can make a start on the packing."

A couple of hours later, Ginny and I had managed to scrape together a couple of boxes, mostly linens with a few books and games, and a few toys that had belonged to Jerry and me as children. It really was a paltry offering. I was glad Ginny had volunteered to see what she had too.

"Well, I suppose it's time I made that telephone call," I said.

But before I could do so, it rang. It was DI Wilkes for Albert. Ginny, Jerry and I stood in the background listening to one side of the conversation.

"Hello?"

"Ah, Samuel, what's the latest?"

"They can't?"

"No, I see."

"Good idea. Yes, see what you can find and we'll go from there."

"Of course, will do."

"Yes, I'm heading back shortly and will update you then. It'll probably be tomorrow. Just awaiting confirmation."

"Of course. Cheerio."

Albert replaced the receiver and turned to us all, notebook and pencil in hand.

"That was DI Wilkes with an update. Our man in Yorkshire wasted no time upon arrival. Talked to the local constabulary and the witnesses, and visited what was left of the crime scene." He paused, sighing.

Ginny had her arms crossed and was impatiently tapping her foot. "Uncle Albert, please just get on with it. Was it him?"

"Actually," I said, "would you mind if I made that call first? I'd rather do it before Albert tells us what he knows."

"Of course not, you go ahead and I'll make some tea. We can meet in the drawing room shortly." Then she turned on her heel toward the kitchen.

I took the card Jerry had given me and went to the telephone. Taking a deep breath, I dialled and waited for someone to pick up. I had expected a secretary to answer so was surprised into sudden silence when I heard Peter's voice boom in my ear.

"Peter Clairmont, good morning."

"Hello? Is there anybody there?"

Gathering both my wits and my courage, I managed to answer. "Peter, it's Ella."

"Ella, hello. Well, I must say I didn't expect it to be you. Are you well?"

"I'm very well, Peter, thank you. I hope I'm not interrupting anything?"

"No, not at all. Just some paperwork. How can I help?"

"I just wondered if it would be convenient for me to come tomorrow with the donations?"

"Goodness, that was quick work. I didn't expect you to have it done already."

"Oh, well, it was good timing for me actually. I'm still unpacking, remember, so it was no trouble."

"Ah, of course. Well, I'm tied up in meetings in the morning but I'm free around noon if that works for you. Would you like me to come and get them... save you the journey?"

"Oh, no, that's quite all right, Peter, I've already arranged for some help. Noon is fine. I'll see you then."

"Yes, all right, see you then."

I hung up and leaned against the wall for a moment. I hadn't realised how nervous I would be and my heart was pounding. I just hoped I'd sounded sincere and calm. Although, if that was the result of a simple telephone conversation, it didn't bode well for my meeting him face-to-face.

I shrugged the thought off. No point worrying about it now the appointment was made and the plan was in motion.

Moving into the drawing room, I sat and helped myself to tea. I turned as Albert began speaking.

"As I was saying, my man in Yorkshire has been very busy in the short time he has been there. Unfortunately, we still have nothing concrete. Mr. Peter Clairmont Senior was a widower. Lived alone and was a very private man. Kept himself to himself and rarely ventured out, except to go to church. He had no live-in staff, just a daily who was a maid-of-all-work. Consequently my man's finding it difficult to track down anyone who knew him."

"So we're no further forward. We can't say for certain that our man was even there except for the identification card in his wallet, which he could have got from a third party," sighed Jerry.

"Well, certainly at the moment that's the lie of the land. However, my man is still digging up there, so all is not lost," Albert added.

"But without definitive proof it still means Ella will have to go and see Peter tomorrow, won't it?" asked Ginny.

"Only if she's comfortable doing so, Ginny, as I said before," answered Albert. "We're on the case and if there's something to find then we'll find it. My gut feeling is that our man was involved. But if you want to expedite matters then this is currently the best option we have, yes."

Albert rose and stood in front of the mantel.

"There is one interesting piece of information he found though. One woman witness, a member of the same church as the deceased, remembers him mentioning a niece who died as a child."

"Mary!" gasped Ginny.

"That was my first thought," said Albert. "She also said he mentioned that the sister was a 'bad lot.'"

I frowned. "That doesn't make sense. How would he know that if she died at the orphanage?"

"To be honest, Ella, my man was of the opinion that this woman was confused and probably thinking of someone else. She's very old and not the most reliable of witnesses sadly. 'Losing her marbles' was the way he described her."

I nodded. That seemed the most logical explanation.

"DI Wilkes is trying to find photographic evidence of our Peter Clairmont. We can show it around up there and see if anyone recognises him," Albert continued.

"Well, I can help with that," said Jerry. "There was a reporter from the Times at the fundraiser. It was a rather large society event, you know, so quite a lot of well-known faces. There was a spot in the paper about it. I daresay the photographer that was with him got several shots."

"Excellent thinking, Jerry. I'll call Wilkes back and let him know," said Albert, who was once again scribbling in his little black book.

I stood up, smoothing down my skirt.

"Well, if everyone is ready, I think the best thing is to head up to London now. There's still a lot to do before tomorrow."

Fifteen minutes later the car was packed and we were heading over the bridge to the mainland. This time tomorrow, I thought, I'd be entering the lion's den.

CHAPTER THIRTEEN

En route back to London in Albert's car, the conversation naturally continued where we had left off.

More than once I was asked if I still wanted to go through with the plan. And if I were being honest with myself, I was beginning to have second thoughts. Mainly because, like Albert, I too had a gut feeling that Peter Clairmont was involved in the death of the man in Yorkshire.

But then my meditations turned to Milly and her need for justice. I had to continue on my path for her sake, otherwise she would never find peace. And aside from that, if I didn't, I would have a ghost in my house forever. Terrific fun at gatherings, I'll admit, but hardly fair.

No. I'd been chosen for a reason and I had to believe that reason would also mean a positive outcome.

"I think Milly found out, you know." I said.

"What do you mean?" said Jerry, turning to face Ginny and me in the back seat.

"I've no doubt now that Milly brought that wallet to me in the hopes I'd realise what the card inside meant. I believe she found out Peter Clairmont was an impostor. And he had to silence her."

"That poor child," said Ginny. "She must have been terrified."

"There's something else too. I can't make sense of why he told us he'd once lived at the orphanage," I said, perplexed.

"Did he not explain that? Because his parents died?" Ginny asked. "Also the reason he was working there was because of the girl that died."

"That's what he said Ginny, yes. But why say it? The man he is supposed to be impersonating wasn't an orphan."

Ginny continued to look confused, but Jerry latched on right away.

"Of course! You think he let it slip by accident?"

I nodded. "I think he must have. I think he let his guard down when he was with us all for lunch and it slipped out. At that point it was too late to retract the information. So he told a little more and then I suspect he hoped we'd think it unimportant and forget about it."

"Which we would have done had it not been for Milly," said Jerry. "But, of course, he doesn't know about her."

"Exactly," I said.

"I'm not sure I follow," said Ginny. "Are you saying he was an orphan, or he wasn't?"

"Oh, I'm sure he was. But we know it wasn't under the name Peter Clairmont. He told us by accident, Ginny. And by doing so he blew his cover."

"Good heavens!" Ginny cried. "I understand now. I've always said that if you lie you'll get found out. It's so easy to lose track and trip yourself up. I wonder if the other staff realise he's not who he says he is?"

That startled me. I'd never given a thought to the other staff, so focused was I on Milly and our suspect.

"That's an angle my men and I are pursuing, Ginny. Ella, that was a fine piece of detective work. You too, Jerry."

"Thank you, old boy. It just goes to show that Peter isn't as clever as he thinks he is. He's already made one crucial mistake. What's the betting he'll make another?"

"I agree," Albert nodded. "And I'll even stick my neck out and say I do believe we're one step ahead of our quarry."

We were soon to find out just how wrong Albert was.

Once back at the apartment, Jerry disappeared to work on his latest manuscript. Apparently, this 'Clairmont Caper' as he'd dubbed it, had given him a wealth of new ideas.

An hour later he popped his head round the door of Ginny's dressing room, where he found us practically buried beneath huge mounds of linens and clothing.

"Good grief, Ginny, are we moving out?" he asked.

"Of course not, Jerry. Ella and I are sorting out things for the orphanage."

I actually wasn't doing much sorting at all. So far all I'd done was barely catch the various items Ginny had thrown from drawers and cupboards. I was amazed at just how much these seemingly small items of furniture could hold. It was like an optical illusion.

Jerry eyed a silk and sequinned evening gown. "I'm not sure that frock would be appropriate."

"Don't be silly, Jerry. That's for Ella," Ginny's muffled voice said from the depths of the wardrobe.

"Ah, of course. Well, here's the book. I'll just put it here, shall I?" he said, eying a particularly precarious pile.

"Yes, of course, dear, that's fine," Ginny said, without looking up.

Needless to say, as soon as he put it down the whole lot teetered for a second before toppling and crashing down in a great avalanche, finally coming to rest an inch before my feet.

"Ah. Right. Jolly good. Well, I'll leave you to it then, shall I?" Jerry said and, making a hasty retreat, went back to his writing.

Ginny, having extricated herself from the depths of the closet, turned and looked aghast at the mess.

"Oh, dear. Do you think this is too much?" she asked me.

For a split second, there was absolute silence, then I burst into peals of laughter. I couldn't help it. Collapsing on the nearest soft pile, I gasped, "Ginny, you are a darling, truly. We can barely move in here, I haven't seen the sofa for hours, I'm on the floor and our only exit is blocked."

She came and sat beside me and began to laugh too.

"So you're politely saying there's too much. Well, let's just pack up half that pile over there and call it a day. I'll have Betty sort the rest out later."

That evening, Jerry came into the drawing room where Ginny and I sat talking by the fire.

"I've just seen the collection in the hall. I must say, you girls did a remarkable job getting all that stuff into just three boxes. Well done."

We just looked at each other and smiled. We both loved Jerry dearly but sometimes he seemed to live in a different world.

"So, Ella. How are you feeling about tomorrow?" he asked, handing us both a drink, then sitting in the chair next to mine, while Ginny lounged on the sofa.

"I'm a little nervous. I keep telling myself that Peter doesn't know the real reason I'll be there, but I can't help being affected by what we've uncovered. I also haven't seen Milly or Phantom since dinner last night. I don't quite know what to make of that."

At that moment the telephone rang and Jerry went to answer it.

"That was Uncle Albert," he said when he returned. "Nothing particularly useful to report, I'm afraid. They managed to get an image from the press photographer, but only one. He was in profile in a group of other chaps, so it's not very good. I'm surprised there's not more. My feeling is that he deliberately avoided having his photograph taken. A sign he's hiding something in my opinion. Albert may have some more news on that tomorrow. He also said his man Jimmy would be here with a car around 11:30 in the morning. That gives us time to pack everything up and for Ella to be there by noon."

"Did he say anything about the other orphanage staff?" I asked.

Jerry shook his head. "Not in so many words. He's spoken to those in charge, the ones that hired Peter. But according to their paperwork, references and so on, Peter Clairmont is an upstanding character and above reproach."

"Well, of course he would be, wouldn't he?" I said, exasperated. "But it's not Peter Clairmont they've given the job to."

"No. It sounds as though they don't know he's an impostor. From what Albert said he's digging a little deeper, but doesn't want to scupper your attempts tomorrow. It's important Peter doesn't get wind of what's going on. Albert's primary concern is your safety at this point, Ella."

I doubted I would sleep at all that night but knew I needed to get as much rest as possible. I needed to have my wits about me to meet Peter Clairmont. The man was clever. I just hoped I could match his cleverness.

CHAPTER FOURTEEN

B y the time I got down to the car the next morning, Jimmy
Smith was just loading up the last of the boxes. He was a
slightly rotund man, short, with a shock of unruly brown
hair just beginning to grey at the temples.

"Good morning, Miss," he said, whilst dabbing a sweating brow
with a handkerchief. He was rather red in the face and I was concerned he'd over-exerted himself.

"Good morning, Mr. Smith. Are you quite all right?"

"Oh, yes, Miss, nothing to worry about. Just getting over a slight
cold, that's all. Are you ready to go?"

I turned and gave Ginny and Jerry a quick wave, then got in
the car. We'd already said our goodbyes back in the apartment.
Ginny was rather tearful so I insisted she stay inside. Jerry gave me
a quick hug.

"Now be careful, old girl. No taking any chances."

I assured him I wouldn't.

It wasn't very far to the orphanage but the traffic was particularly heavy, so the journey took a little longer than expected. Mr. Smith and I spent the time going over the details.

"I expect there will be someone to help you unload the boxes at the other end," I said. "Perhaps Peter will offer."

"Well, I daresay that'll be true, miss, but I'd rather do it myself. I'm here as a paid delivery man so I need to keep up the charade."

"Yes, of course, I understand. But you will be inside with me, won't you?"

"Oh, yes. I've been given strict instructions not to let you out of my sight."

I smiled. It seemed as though Albert had thought of everything and it gave me a sense of relief to know I wouldn't be alone.

As we pulled up in front of the orphanage, we found Peter Clairmont standing at the door waiting for us.

"He's a bit keen, isn't he?" Jimmy commented under his breath. "Well, this is it, miss. Keep calm and don't worry. I'll be right there with you."

I nodded, thanked Jimmy and, taking a deep breath, exited the car. I glanced round briefly to see if I could spot Albert's men, but while I knew they were there, they were very well hidden.

"Hello, Peter, I do apologise for being late but the traffic was terrible."

"Not to worry, Ella. I've the rest of the afternoon off actually so it makes no difference."

Jimmy came over, cap in hand and looked at Peter. "Where do you want these boxes then, gov?"

I winced, wondering if Jimmy was over-playing his part, but Peter didn't seem to notice.

"You can put them in the common room. First door on the left," Peter said, pointing. As Jimmy came over, struggling with one of the boxes, I waited for Peter to offer his help. He didn't. But as luck would have it the common room was exactly where I wanted to be.

"I'll show you the way, Mr. Smith." I said. I'd decided I had to be a little more demonstrative. I didn't want Peter to take control. My plan was to be in and out as quickly as possible and if Peter were allowed to take charge it might take far longer. Plus I might not be successful in obtaining the information I sought. No, I had to force his hand.

With new determination, I marched up the steps with Peter at my side and Jimmy huffing and puffing behind me.

"Oh, I've just remembered, Peter. Jerry sent this for you." I handed him a small parcel wrapped in brown paper and tied with string. While he was opening it, I moved into the common room and wandered down to the display case at the end.

"Well, I must say this is very kind of Jerry. A signed copy of his latest novel. I haven't got around to purchasing it yet. I'll look forward to reading it."

"Yes, he thought you'd like it. I'll let him know how pleased you are," I said, gazing in the cabinet.

"Is there something in particular you're looking for in there?" Peter asked, and I wondered if I'd imagined the sharpness in his tone.

"Not really, no. I just wondered why there were no names listed beside the pictures. It seems strange to remember them in this way but have no names."

"Well, there's a perfectly simple explanation for that. I haven't got around to doing it yet," Peter said.

"Oh, I see," I said, nodding. "Well, perhaps you could tell me their names?"

I could see Peter's reflective frown in the glass of the case and realised I'd not been subtle enough.

"Why do you want to know, Ella?"

Oh, dear. This wasn't going to plan at all. I was definitely raising his suspicions. I had to think of something … and fast. I decided an abbreviated version of the truth would be best, even though I had sworn never to mention I'd been married. But I couldn't think of another angle under such pressured circumstances. I made a bit of a show of gathering myself together and then began.

"I'm not sure how much you know about me. Peter, but I'm a widow. John, my husband, died nearly five years ago. We were only married for two years. We had planned on having a family but he was taken from me before …" I sighed and took a handkerchief from my purse. Quickly dabbing my eyes, I replaced it, then looked directly at him.

"I'm sorry. I still find it difficult to talk about. The fact is I've been thinking about these poor children since I first saw them. They seem to have lodged themselves in my heart. Their stories are so sad, especially the poor child that drowned. It seems such a senseless waste of life."

Peter gently laid a hand on my shoulder.

"I'm terribly sorry, Ella. I didn't realise what you'd been through. Of course, I now understand why this would affect you so much. Look, I have all the old records in my office. Come on, we can go through them together."

As we walked back to the other end of the room, we found Jimmy patiently sitting on a chair. He'd moved all the boxes already and was waiting for me.

"Thank you, Mr. Smith, you can go now. I'll see Miss Bridges safely back."

I shot a panicked glance at Jimmy—this wouldn't do at all.

"Oh, well, I can't do that, I'm afraid, sir. The lady has hired me for a full day's work, you see."

Oh well done, Jimmy! I thought. *Very quick thinking.*

"Is that so?" Peter asked, looking at me. I could see immediately that he was terribly annoyed although was trying to hide it.

"Yes, it is. I have several other errands to run, which Mr. Smith is kindly helping me with. You won't mind waiting, Jimmy, while Peter and I go through some old records?"

"Of course not, miss. You go ahead with the gentleman and I'll wait here for you." He then produced a series of particularly loud sneezes.

"Oh, dear. Are you sure you'll be all right?" I asked. I was becoming increasingly concerned that his cold was a little more serious than he was letting on.

"No need to worry about me, I'll be fine. 'Tis just a bit of a cold, that's all."

"I'll have some tea brought out to you, Mr. Smith. That should warm you up a bit while you wait. Unfortunately the heating isn't working at the moment," Peter said.

"That's very kind of you, sir, thank you."

Peter nodded and then turned on his heel towards the office. I smiled briefly at Jimmy, who returned it with a wink, then set off in Peter's wake. Very soon I would have the information Albert needed and we could leave.

When I got to the office, Peter wasn't there. I was wondering where on earth he'd got to when he came in behind me and I nearly jumped out of my skin. "I've just ordered some tea for us and your man. Shouldn't be long. Please have a seat."

He gestured to the only comfortable piece of furniture in the room—a club chair, upholstered in soft, green damask. It looked incredibly out of place in such an austere setting. The rest of the office by contrast was dark and gloomy. With no window to let in any natural light the only source of illumination was a desk lamp. It was thoroughly depressing. Much like what I'd seen in the rest of the building. I could only suppose this chair had been a recent donation.

As Peter was rifling through an oak filing cabinet, the door opened and a tray of tea was brought in by the maid.

"Ah, Maude, thank you. Would you be so kind as to take a cup to Mr. Smith? He's in the common room."

"Of course, sir." She picked up an already filled cup and, with a brief glance at me, left, closing the door behind her.

Peter filled the other two cups from the teapot and left me to add my own milk and sugar. He returned to the cabinet, periodically taking a folder and placing it on a small pile.

Just as he was turning several minutes later, files in hand, a breathless and panicked Maude crashed into the room.

"Oh, Mr. Clairmont sir, you better come quick. That gentleman wot was in the common room 'as collapsed!"

"What?" I ran out with Peter, who was yelling for Maude to fetch the Matron.

I found Jimmy on the floor, unconscious, but breathing.

The Matron must have been nearby because she was suddenly at my side, examining him.

"He'll be all right. He's just fainted. But he's running a slight temperature. Maude and I will take him to the infirmary and get him settled. Do you know if he's been ill?" This directed at me.

"He mentioned that he was just getting over a cold, but that's all I know."

She nodded. "Well, that would do it. He's obviously done too much. Ah, look, he's coming round."

I glanced down and Jimmy's eyes were fluttering.

"Maude, help me get him in the chair."

I hadn't heard Maude come back, but she moved into view, wheeling a wicker chair.

Jimmy focused on my face. "Sorry about this, miss. I'll be all right in a couple of minutes."

"It doesn't matter in the slightest, Mr. Smith. Matron's going to take you to the infirmary…"

Jimmy began to protest, which resulted in a coughing fit.

"I'll have no argument now. You need to rest and it's only for a short while. Matron will take care of you until you're feeling better. I'd be much happier knowing you are all right. I'll be along shortly."

He nodded, looking highly embarrassed, but resigned to his fate.

As I watched Matron and Maude wheel Jimmy away, I felt a hand on my elbow. I jumped, having forgotten Peter was there in my worry.

"He'll be all right, Ella, he's in good hands. Let's go back to the office and finish our tea. By then Matron will have Mr. Smith settled and I'll take you to him."

CHAPTER FIFTEEN

B
ack at the office, having hurriedly finished my tea, I grabbed my bag. Turning, I noticed Peter was putting back the files.

"Perhaps we could take those along with us?" I suggested. Although Jimmy was at the forefront of my concerns, I hadn't lost sight of the real reason I had come. I needed to see those files.

"That won't be possible, I'm afraid. It's policy the files don't leave the office. However, we'll come back after we've been to the infirmary and go through them. I'm sure by the time we get there, Mr. Smith will have recovered."

"Yes, of course, I'm sure you're right," I said, smiling.

As Peter locked the office door, I turned to go in the direction Matron had gone, but Peter turned the opposite way.

"We'll go this way. It's the staff entrance and much quicker."

He strode down the corridor, turned left and opened a door at the end of another hallway, gesturing me to go through first. We entered what looked like a schoolroom, with a chalkboard on the wall and twenty small desks and chairs. All were empty. Peter locked the door and then proceeded to another at the far end of the room.

"Are there no classes today?" I asked.

"No, the children and staff are all out on a trip to the museum."

As I exited the classroom, I found myself in yet another corridor.

"This building is much larger than I thought," I said nervously. I didn't like how things were progressing. It felt very much like the lion's den Jerry had mentioned.

Peter smiled. "Yes, it's a veritable maze and very easy to get lost if you don't know where you're going."

"How far is it? We seemed to have been walking rather a long time," I asked. It wasn't the short cut Peter had intimated.

"Just through that door in front."

At that moment a streak of black shot past me and stopped at the door, hissing at us. Phantom! This was definitely a warning.

I stopped. "Actually, Peter, I think I'd like to go back now. I've just remembered I was supposed to meet Ginny. She'll worry if I'm not there."

He stopped with his hands on his hips, looking at the floor. He was shaking his head and laughing in a sarcastic way. Looking up, he came towards me and grabbed my upper arm in a vice-like grip.

"Did anyone ever tell you, Ella, you are an appalling liar?"

"Peter, that hurts, and what do you mean I'm lying? I can assure you I'm not. Please let go of my arm this instant."

"I think not, dear Ella. You're coming with me," and he dragged me to the door. I fought as hard as I could but he was too strong. As he pushed me through the doorway I heard a click and a light came on. In front were a series of steps heading down. It was a basement. I took a step back and felt something sharp dig into my lower back.

"One single word and I will shoot. Do you understand?"

Oh, my God, he had a gun! What an idiot I'd been. I couldn't believe how badly Jerry, Ginny, Albert and I had underestimated Peter.

"Please," I whimpered, barely recognising my own voice.

I felt him grab my hair and wrench my head back. I let out an involuntary cry of pain.

"This is your last warning, Ella. One more peep out of you and I will kill you. Now move!" He jabbed the gun into my spine.

I took a faltering step forward and slowly began to descend the stairs, tears trickling down my face. It was like descending an abyss into hell and I'd never been more scared in my entire life.

At the bottom of the stairs, Peter pushed me roughly to the right and turned on another light. We were in the boiler room. There were huge pipes running along the walls and disappearing up through the ceiling. To the left was an old sink and on the right a huge unlit furnace. Stacked against the walls were a myriad of broken items; several bedsteads and mattresses, chairs missing legs and wicker baskets with gaping holes. Everywhere had a layer of black soot. It was dark, cold and filthy.

But what frightened me more than anything was the single, solitary chair set in the middle of the room.

It was an old dentist's chair. A black and chrome monstrosity that spoke of untold pain, but horrifically it had been adapted. It now looked like an instrument of torture.

"No," I whispered and backed away. The barrel of the gun was once more cruelly shoved into my back.

"Yes," Peter whispered malevolently in my ear.

The chair was made from metal but had a worn black leather seat, back, arms and headrest. Attached to the arms and the head were thick restraints. He meant to strap me down! I couldn't let him do it, for as soon as I was strapped in I would never escape. I would be at the mercy of a killer. But what could I do? I had to think, and quickly.

As I was about to speak I heard a voice calling from above—salvation!

"Help! Down here! Please help me," I cried.

I felt sudden pain as Peter backhanded me across the face and I fell to the floor. I could taste blood in my mouth and I felt sick and dizzy. The pain was excruciating and I prayed I wouldn't pass out.

I felt myself lifted bodily and thrown in the chair. Before I could recover my senses my worst fears came true and I was crudely restrained.

I thought my shouts had been in vain, but then I heard someone coming down the steps. *Thank goodness.*

"Look out, he's got a gun," I shouted in warning to whoever was coming to my rescue. I didn't want them to get hurt too.

"For god's sake, can't you keep her quiet?" said a voice. As she rounded the corner I saw it was the Matron.

"Why aren't you with Mr. Smith?" demanded Peter.

"Calm down, I've given him another sedative. Combined with the one I slipped into his tea he'll be out for hours, and I've sent Maude home. It's just you and me, dear brother."

Brother?

"Ah, look, the light has dawned. Yes, this is my sister," Peter said with a twisted smile.

Suddenly it began to make sense. The woman from the church in Yorkshire saying the sister was 'a bad lot.' She was no more senile than I was, but no one had taken her seriously.

I realised then just how hopeless my situation was. There was no way to escape with the two of them against me. But I wasn't going to die not knowing the truth.

"I thought Mary was your sister?"

Matron stared at Peter. "You told her?"

"No, of course not. She must have guessed. Didn't I tell you she was poking around asking too many questions? It would seem our dear Ella here has pieced together more than we thought."

"Peter, I really don't understand. I hardly know anything. You're right when you say I guessed Mary was your sister, but that was only because you seemed more upset about her than the others. It was a tragic accident. But what does that have to do with me?"

Peter cocked his head to one side and I could see he was deciding whether or not to believe me. Perhaps I was getting through.

"Well, unfortunately, Ella, even if I did believe you had simply made a clever guess, the fact now is you do know too much."

I stared at him, my heart beating a wild staccato in my throat. He had no idea how much I had pieced together but he would find out soon enough. I did know too much and I realised what he said was true. He couldn't possibly let me go now. There and then I resolved to get some answers. To do what I had set out to do: learn the truth for Milly's sake.

"Is that why you killed Millicent? Because she found out you were an impostor? That the real Peter Clairmont died in a fire eighteen months ago?"

Two single strides and he had caught me by the throat. His eyes bored into mine as though he were trying to see my very thoughts. Spittle caught at the corners of his mouth as he roared in my face.

"How do you know about that?"

I shook my head. I couldn't breathe, let alone speak.

"You're choking her. How is she supposed to answer you?"

Peter glanced back at his sister, then released my throat. I coughed and tried to catch my breath.

"I'll ask you again. How do you know so much, Ella?"

I heard a click as Peter cocked the hammer on the gun and levelled it at my heart.

"I'll tell you if you put the gun away and answer one question."

"I hardly think you're in a position to bargain," he said.

"I have nothing to lose, Peter," I replied. "You're the one holding the gun and I'm the one strapped to a chair. You're going to kill me anyway. I'd just like to know if I was right before I die."

He laughed. It was almost maniacal. Not like the quietly reserved Peter I had thought he was. I felt revulsion that I had ever liked him at all.

"Of course, you are right. I do in fact hold all the cards." He lowered the gun. "And I suppose I could grant your last wish, seeing as though you so cleverly put it all together. However, I need to know who else you told. It makes no difference obviously because they'll never find your body, and we'll be long gone by the time anyone realises you are missing. However, I find it's always good to know who your enemies are. Just in case. It helps me sleep at night. So, who else knows?"

"No one," I said. I would not risk my family.

He leaned against a pipe with his arms folded, the gun casually resting on his forearm, one leg crossed over the other. He looked, to all intents and purposes, as though he were having a casual conversation in a club, rather than kidnapping me and planning a murder.

"Now, you see, I can tell you are lying with that statement, Ella. But no matter. It's obvious you would have discussed this with your brother and his wife. I know how close you are."

"Don't you dare hurt them," I shouted. "They don't know anything. They believe I came here to donate for the children and that's all. Do you think Jerry would have given you his book if he had any inclination who you really are?"

I was scared out of my wits. But now I was also angry, and this seemed to make my story ring true.

"Well, well, well. I do believe you're telling the truth this time. Good girl."

"Now it's your turn," I said. "Did you kill Millicent because she discovered the truth?"

"That child was as irritating as you. Always sticking her nose in where it didn't belong, and one day she went too far. She found out all right and I couldn't risk her blabbing, I had to shut her up. Of course I killed her, but what I want to know is how you found out?"

I'd done it. He'd confessed and now I knew the truth. I exhaled and smiled.

"You'd never believe it."

"Try me," he said.

"Milly told me."

As soon as I spoke those words utter chaos broke out.

Milly appeared right in front of me. Matron screamed and took a step back, right under a shelf where Phantom was waiting. With one swipe of his paw he dislodged a heavy can, which landed on her head, knocking her out instantly. As she crumpled to the floor, Peter took a step back, utter shock registering on his face. He tripped over an abandoned case, banging his head on the pipe behind and slid to the ground, unconscious.

The gun clattered to the floor and discharged a bullet, which ricocheted off the sink and embedded itself in a water pipe, which promptly burst, spraying foul-smelling brown liquid everywhere. Then a voice shouted from the stairs.

"This is the police! Stay where you are!"

As several men, led by Jimmy, came rushing down into the room, I caught sight of Milly. She smiled, nodded and then, giving me a small wave, slowly faded from view.

CHAPTER SIXTEEN

A few hours later, the four of us were back where we started. Snug in front of the fire in the drawing room of my cottage. It was so very good to be home again.

"So tell me again how Jimmy escaped," I asked Albert.

"Well, of course, he realised at once that his tea had been drugged. He'd only drunk a small amount at that point, and with a spot of quick thinking he poured the remainder away. Once he heard Maude returning, he quickly lay as though passed out."

"He looked terrible when I found him there," I said. "I was so worried."

"Well, it wasn't as bad as it could have been. He was dizzy and disoriented of course, but he did a remarkable job under those circumstances."

"So what happened in the infirmary?" Jerry asked.

Albert continued. "Well, as you know, Matron told Peter she had given him another sedative. She also mentioned that she'd sent Maude home."

I nodded.

"Jimmy knew the likelihood of being drugged again. He realised you were the one they wanted, Ella, and they were making sure he was out of the way. This time the drug was in hot milk, which Matron prepared. She told Jimmy to drink it up whilst she walked Maude to the door, having given her the rest of the afternoon off. During that time, Jimmy poured away the milk and then pretended to be in a deep sleep, which is exactly what Matron saw when she returned. She had no reason to think Jimmy suspected anything."

"So was Maude involved in these shenanigans?" Ginny asked.

Albert shook his head. "Not at all. The tea had already been prepared by Matron. Maude was just following instructions."

"So how did Jimmy find out where I had been taken?"

"He followed Matron, right, Albert?" Jerry asked.

"He did indeed," confirmed Albert. "Once he knew where you were being kept, he came and warned the men I'd posted outside. DI Wilkes then came and got me."

"Goodness. He did very well finding his way around the place. I was hopelessly lost within a couple of minutes," I said.

"Well, as I said, Ella, I gave you my best man. Jimmy spent a number of years as a beat officer and knows the London streets like the back of his hand. A few corridors in the orphanage, if you'll forgive the pun, were like child's play."

I rose and went to the liquor cabinet where I refreshed everyone's drinks.

"So did you hear Peter's confession? How he murdered poor Milly?" I asked.

Albert shook his head. "Not at the time. We'd arrived too late for that, I'm afraid. All we heard was a loud crash and a gunshot. That's when we rushed in."

"Oh, no," cried Ginny. "Do you mean to say that Ella's heroic actions have all been in vain?"

"Not at all, Ginny. Both Peter and his sister have been singing like songbirds since we picked them up. We know much more than we ever did. Peter not only confessed to killing Milly, but also to killing the real Peter Clairmont, who it turns out was actually their uncle."

"But I thought he was in Ireland," I said.

"He was. It's where Peter and his sister grew up. That much was true. However, they moved back to Yorkshire a couple of years ago, after Mr. Clairmont's wife died. It was *her* family that was Irish. Once she'd passed away, the old man decided to spend the remainder of his years where he grew up, in Yorkshire."

"But how is it possible that the neighbours didn't know Peter or his sister?" Ginny asked.

This was something that was troubling me too. Surely, if they'd all come over together then they would have been seen, and then I realised the truth.

"They didn't come back with the old man, did they?"

"No, they didn't," said Albert. "There had been a huge disagreement among them all. The old man didn't want anything more to do with them. Called his niece 'a bad lot' and warned his nephew that they'd both get into serious trouble one day. But I think he underestimated how close they were, and how inherently bad."

"So when did they come back, and to where?" Jerry asked.

"Not long after their uncle actually. But they moved into the next village some miles away. There they made plans to kill him. In their minds he had done them a grave wrong, even though he and his wife had brought them both up as their own."

"But I don't understand how they could have financed all of this," said Ginny.

"Actually, that's what I was going on to tell you. There's much more to this pair than we thought. Initially, they used the inheritance they received from their parents, but that was quite meagre and ran out quickly. After that they took to robbery."

"What?" we all exclaimed.

"Oh, yes," Albert said with a huge grin. "It turns out, Ella, that you are responsible for catching two of the most-wanted criminals this country has ever seen."

CHAPTER SEVENTEEN

A few days later, I was sitting having my breakfast and perusing the paper. Albert's news had taken us all by complete surprise. It turned out that Peter and Matron were really Arthur and Mildred Stone, the heads of the notorious Semaphore Gang, so dubbed as the police believed this was their main method of communication. They were responsible for a number of violent robberies up and down the country and a huge manhunt had been underway for months. But it had brought little in the way of clues and the authorities were fast losing hope that they'd ever be caught. That, of course, was before Milly came on the scene.

Jerry, Ginny, and Albert had all said they would never have put me in harm's way like that had they known with whom we were dealing. I very much appreciated their love and concern, but also knew in my heart that it had played out exactly as it was meant to. Milly and Phantom were there all along to see that no harm would befall me.

I glanced at the vase in the centre of the table. It held a single flower—one that was impossible to get at this time of year—a beautiful red poppy. It had been waiting on the table for me after I'd said goodbye to Albert, Ginny, and Jerry. I think it was Milly's way of saying thank you and I knew I would probably never see her again. She was at peace now.

A loud crash from the downstairs pantry shook me back to reality. Phantom, on the other hand, was still around. I went to investigate.

"Oh! Look at the mess, Phantom. What on earth did you do this for?" He was crouched on the top shelf looking down at the smashed eggs and spilled cocoa with glee. He gave a silent meow and disappeared. I sighed and went to look for something to clean it up.

As I was crouched under the sink the telephone rang. It was Ginny.

"Ella, darling, how are you? I hope you don't mind me calling, but Jerry and I went to dinner with some friends last night. And Lady Davenport, I'm sure I've mentioned her to you—told me about a little problem she's been having."

Oh, dear, I didn't like the sound of this at all.

"Well, of course I mentioned you, and …"

"What sort of problem, Ginny?" I interrupted.

"Well, the ghostly kind of course, silly."

"Oh, Ginny, you didn't!"

"Well, of course I did."

I sighed.

"The fact is you have an incredible gift, courtesy of Mrs. Rose, and I have friends who are willing to pay a lot of money for your services."

"Really?" I asked, surprised, then realised I sounded like I was encouraging her and frowned.

"Of course, you'll be highly sought after once word gets around, you know…" She paused, and my heart sank to my stomach. "… Lady Davenport wants to have a séance."

"No, Ginny. Absolutely not."

"Oh, don't be a spoilsport, darling. It'll be fun."

"Ginny, I'm not being a spoilsport. This is not something I would feel comfortable doing. Firstly, I have no doubt that the experience with Milly was a one-off. She's gone now, at peace, thank goodness. But I doubt very much I have a 'gift' as you call it. Secondly, what do you suppose would happen at a séance if I did have a gift? Have you thought of that?"

"Whatever do you mean, darling?"

"I mean, if I am a 'conduit' or whatever you call it for ghosts, how many do you think would appear? It could be hundreds. And what if they are unfriendly, like poltergeists or something? Not only would it be chaos, it could very well be dangerous."

"Oh, dear. Yes, I suppose you're right. What a shame. But what shall I tell Lady Davenport? She'll be so disappointed. She's already talking to the caterers."

"Well, Ginny, really!" I said, exasperated. She'd obviously told Lady Davenport I'd do it. "Just tell her I'm still recovering. But under no circumstances will I ever consider a séance. And please, Ginny, don't promise her, or anyone else for that matter, that I'll be able to deal with their ghosts. I am quite certain it was a one-time incident."

Suitably mollified, Ginny agreed. We spoke for a little while longer and with promises to meet for lunch later in the week, we said goodbye.

I set to cleaning up the mess that Phantom had made in the pantry.

Whilst it was called a pantry, it was more like a small corridor set off from the kitchen with floor to ceiling shelves on either side. These were very deep and it wasn't until a short while later I understood why. Directly in front was another set of shelves, again floor to ceiling, but these were much narrower in depth. Rather like a bookshelf.

As I was on my hands and knees cleaning up the last of the spillage, I noticed a small hole to the side of the narrower shelves. It was perfectly round and at first I thought it must have been made by a mouse. But on closer inspection it was obviously too small and too perfect.

I pondered it for a while then did what anyone would do in the same circumstances. I stuck my finger inside. There was a gentle click as I depressed a lever and the whole shelving unit moved sideways by an inch.

I stood up in shock, staring at the gap that had appeared on the right. A cool draught was blowing through that smelled of old dust and stale air.

Gingerly, I reached out and slid the shelving sideways, and as it slid back it fitted neatly down the edge like a sliding door. So this was why the shelving on either side was so deep. The door was perfectly hidden if you didn't know it was there.

I took a tentative step forward and found myself in a secret room. It was reminiscent of an old banqueting hall, with dark wood-panelled walls, dark oak parquet floor and an iron candelabra hanging from the ceiling. I noticed there were also matching wall sconces, although the candles had long since melted.

In the middle of the room were a large table and chairs that could have seated forty people, and it was fully set for a grand dinner, right down to the floral centre-pieces. These, of course, had long since perished and everything was coated in a thick layer of dust. I couldn't begin to wonder how long it had all been there, nor why the room had been closed off.

Glancing to my right, at the far end of the room I noticed a large dresser, replete with serving dishes, and in the corner two high-backed red velvet upholstered chairs beside a small occasional table in front of a fireplace.

Whilst I was in shock at discovering such a secret in my cottage, what happened next nearly made my heart stop.

A figure leaned forward in one of the chairs and slowly rose to face me.

It looked as though Ginny was right. I did have a gift after all.

ABOUT THE AUTHOR

J. New is the author of The Yellow Cottage Vintage Mysteries, traditional English whodunits with a twist, set in the 1930's. Known for their clever humour as well as the interesting slant on the traditional whodunit, they have all achieved Bestseller status on Amazon.

J. New also writes the Finch and Fischer contemporary cozy crime series and (coming in 2021) the Will Sharpe Mysteries set in her hometown during the 1960's. Her books have sold over one hundred-thousand copies worldwide.

Jacquie was born in West Yorkshire, England. She studied art and design and after qualifying began work as an interior designer, moving onto fine art restoration and animal portraiture before making the decision to pursue her lifelong ambition to write. She now writes full time and lives with her partner of twenty-one years, two dogs and five cats, all of whom she rescued.

••‹‹‹◆›››••

If you enjoyed *An Accidental Murder*, please consider leaving a review on Amazon.

If you would like to be kept up to date with new releases from J. New, you can sign up to her *Reader's Group* on her website www.jnewwrites.com You will also receive a link to download the free e-book, *The Yellow Cottage Mystery*, the short-story prequel to the series.

BOOKS BY J. NEW

The Yellow Cottage Vintage Mysteries in order:

The Yellow Cottage Mystery (Free)
An Accidental Murder
The Curse of Arundel Hall
A Clerical Error
The Riviera Affair
A Double Life

The Finch & Fischer Mysteries in order:

Decked in the Hall
Death at the Duck Pond

Made in the USA
Las Vegas, NV
08 June 2023

73143399R00073